NOCO WRITERS IN QUARANTINE

*BY MEMBERS OF THE
NOCO (NORTH COLUMBIA CITY)
WRITERS WORKSHOP
at OLA WYOLA BOUTIQUE
Organized by ELAINE BONOW*

SEATTLE USA

Cover design by Ren Felman
Organized by Elaine Bonow
Edited and designed by Clark Humphrey

•

First edition: April 2021

ISBN (this edition): 978-1929069-31-6

MISCmedia
1901 Western Ave., #104
Seattle WA 98101

NoCo (North Columbia City) Writers Workshop
c/o Ola Wyola Boutique
4427 Rainier Ave. S.
Seattle WA 98118

miscmedia.com
olawyola.com
wordpress.com/view/nocowriters.home.blog

from NOCO WRITERS IN QUARANTINE

DAPHNE BELLFLOWER, "Blue Hour":

The gargoyle flexed his wings and scratched his feet with his long pointy nails as Lily stared. She finished her drink, and lit another cigarette. Lung cancer was the least of her concerns anymore.

"You're back," the gargoyle said. His voice was harsh and grating, like worn-out brake pads. "I haven't seen you or anyone else up here for a long time." He stretched his long arms and motioned to the empty city below. "What's going on down there?"

ELAINE BONOW, "That'll Teach You":

By the time he sobers up and figures that if he wants to leave, he'll have to walk out. He'll learn that playing dirty with my little family can be dangerous to assholes like him. I did leave him a note: "Jordy, when you do decide to walk out, be sure to watch out for bears."

REN FELMAN, "Love in the Time of Coronavirus":

"Yes, well, it wasn't him, was it? Tells stories about being malnourished as a child and how he and his mother lived in poverty. Well he's quite the gourmand now! Your maman has always been such a sucker for the 'oppressed.' Oh, Jean-Pierre Bloch is SO oppressed in his deluxe flat in the Seizième. She's charmed by the sob story and impressed by the money. I am not fooled, Nathalie. I am not fooled!"

DALMATIA FLEMING, "The Ellen Chronicles":

"Dad called yesterday. He's coming to town and wants to see us."

"Oh, so the Asshole wants to see us, huh? Like, raising us in a 'hippy Jesus commune' and almost ruining our lives wasn't enough for him, he has to come back and see us? I could go the rest of my life without seeing that pervert again."

"I know, but we could at least meet him. You know I'm not looking forward to it either."

"Yeah, I know."

TOM GAFFNEY, "Cornelius Swims to the Swizzle Stick — III":

He watched her assessing him. While he did not normally see himself as someone who might dazzle while wearing a nice tight wetsuit out for the evening, the night, the bay, the more-than-mist but less-than-drizzle and yet somehow continuous precipitation had rendered him more than usually un-self-conscious. His tuber-shaped shadow caught in the iPhone flashlight did not make his spirits any more moist than they already were.

CLARK HUMPHREY, "Aside From That, They Never Touched":

They took bets on whether she'd show up on camera with big frizzed hair and an online-bought biker jacket, maybe even a Harley logo tank top and fake tattoos (until she can get real ones). They agreed she must have instantly become a biker chick—just like she'd transformed over the years, in the presence of previous boyfriends, into an instant soccer geek, an instant wine snob, and an instant jazz historian.

JOANNE KLEIN, "Green and White Polka Dots":

She was walking home by herself and it was the long sunlight and her impatience to get home to put on her old striped pinafore with the big pockets that she did not notice the man in the car across the street. But he pulled away when she happened to look up, and anyway she wasn't thinking about that.

CONTENTS

DAPHNE BELLFLOWER

Daphne Bellflower is a writer, musician, and collector of vintage fur coats and circus memorabilia. Born in Renton, Washington, Daphne left home at 17 and never looked back. She draws her characters and stories from her experiences living on both coasts and her travels around the world. Her writing influences include Plato, Wallace Stevens, the Archie comics, film noir, and David Lynch. Daphne's perfect day includes biscuits, mimosas, doom-scrolling on her phone, and ordering clothes online that she can't wear until 2022.

REXALL

It was 10:30 in the morning when Elizabeth finally walked out her front door. It was already getting hot. She had woken up later than usual. The couple in the apartment next door had been at it again. They fought until late into the night, and she could still hear the baby cry even after they stopped. Elizabeth didn't fall asleep until dawn. Maybe she would take try to take a nap after she checked her mail.

Elizabeth left the house later than she wanted because she took a long time getting dressed. Her days were her own now, but she still made sure her hair and makeup were perfect. She was pleased with how she looked today, but just wished it had taken less time. She had to get the post office immediately, and then to the bank.

Elizabeth wondered if her heels were too high to run across the boulevard without getting hit by a car. The nearest crosswalk was a long Los Angeles block away. She waited for a break in traffic, took a deep breath and ran across La Brea to the post office.

She smoothed her hair and straightened her dress before she pushed open the tall glass doors. She fished through her purse and found the little key, #224. She opened the brass door and pulled out an envelope, the vellum crisp and smooth. "Elizabeth Chandler," typed impersonally with her new mailing address. Her monthly check had finally arrived. She smiled and slipped the envelope into her purse.

Elizabeth stepped outside and looked around, shielding her face from the sun with her gloved hand. The air smelled sweet, a combination of lemons and gardenias and car exhaust. Elizabeth watched the people and cars navigate Sunset Boulevard. She loved how busy this street was; spontaneous, crowded, alive. This unplanned, unscheduled day stretched ahead of her like a gift.

After a few minutes, she put on more lipstick and walked to the bank. "That's a lot of money, pretty lady," the teller said as she signed the check. Elizabeth looked at his cheap suit, the thin mustache above his leering smile. His small black eyes reminded her of a rat. She shrugged. "Not really," she said. "I'd like $100 in cash, small bills please." She refused to look at him as he laid her bills on the counter. Elizabeth neatly folded the money and put it into her purse. Money was the one unchanged remnant of her discarded life, the only aspect she had ever really liked about it.

In her old life, Elizabeth's days were parsed by meals, appointments and inconsequential tasks. She was married then, but memories of Harry were less vivid than the monotony of her days. Breakfast at 8:00, attend to letters and invitations after breakfast, get dressed for lunches that had been scheduled weeks in advance, tennis or cards depending on the day, get dressed again for dinner at home or at friends, then to bed. Breakfast again at 8:00 the next day. The meals were the only things that ever really changed.

Their house was always dark and quiet, the way Harry liked it. Heavy curtains protected the interior from the blistering Pasadena heat, while the household staff silently picked up the remnants of their meals and Elizabeth's discarded clothes. Her throat always felt tight in that house, like she was going to choke. It was noisy where she lived now, the days and nights were full of the messy sounds of human existence.

Elizabeth decided to go to the drugstore before she returned to her apartment. It amused her, the flashing Rexall sign with a neon arrow pointing to the front door. She walked in and headed to the lunch counter. "Is Dr. Spencer here?" she asked the waitress. "Can you please let him know Elizabeth Chandler is here to see him." She sat on a round red stool to wait. The waitress tightened her lips and walked over to the prescription window. "He's here," she called, motioning to Elizabeth. "He can see you now."

Elizabeth didn't see him at first. She leaned over the prescription counter and saw his bulky body sprawled in a too-small folding chair. He was mopping his sweaty face with a grimy handkerchief. "Hot enough for you?" she asked, laughing. "It's not even noon yet." Dr. Spencer groaned, and with effort pushed himself out of the chair. She could smell alcohol on him, a sharp medicinal scent. He was his own best advertisement for his Prohibition side business.

"I need a bottle of gin," she whispered. "I've got cash." He lumbered to the back room and returned with a rectangular box, wrapped in brown paper and tied with string. Elizabeth never understood why he didn't just put the bottle into a bag, but she didn't want to talk to him any more than she had to. She found Dr. Spencer disgusting, his bad breath, greasy hair, and his stomach hanging over the strained belt of his white pharmacist pants. He smiled as she handed him two $1.00 bills.

"I've got something else you might want," he said quietly,

opening a drawer below the counter. "I got this in Chinatown last week." He pushed a tiny folded packet over the counter. Elizabeth quickly took off her glove, unfolded the envelope, and dabbled the white powder on the tip of her tongue. It tasted acrid and she felt it immediately, a little nausea and then that warm tingling feeling. "How much?," she asked, her face neutral. He'd charge her more if he knew how much she wanted it.

"It's going to be another $3.00," he said. She silently opened her purse, handed him the money, and put the packet in her wallet. This day was turning out even better than she planned. "I've got to go," Elizabeth said, pulling on her glove as she quickly walked away from the counter.

"You forgot your package," Dr. Spencer said. He handed her the box and grabbed her arm. Elizabeth jerked it away from him and took a couple of steps back. "You'd better be careful with that stuff," he hissed. "I don't know how strong it is and I don't want anyone turning up dead. If anything happens, you didn't get it here." He watched her walk out of the store, watched the way her long legs and ass moved under her baby blue dress. He wiped the sweat off the back of his neck and took a drink from the bottle under the counter. It was going to be a long, hot day.

Elizabeth walked back to her apartment building, using the crosswalk this time. The Garden Court was full of people who didn't talk about their past and didn't ask her about hers. She loved it there. Most of the residents were minor movie players or would-be movie players with improbable sounding names. She hadn't met anyone actually from Los Angeles, like she was. They were from all over, from places she'd never heard of and most likely never visit. Kansas City, Tulsa, Yuma, Tacoma.

She was hot after walking up the stairs from the street to her apartment. As she caught her breath, she heard a familiar sound. Her next door neighbor was crying quietly on her front porch, like she did most days after her husband left to look for work. Elizabeth was surprised to see her sitting outside after the commotion last night. She wondered how she could get to her own apartment without having to acknowledge her neighbor.

Elizabeth walked past her quickly, averting her eyes. She put her key in her lock and stopped. "Is your baby asleep?" she asked. The woman looked at her and nodded. Her lip was split and her arms were covered in bruises. "My feet hurt," Elizabeth said. "Can I sit out here with you for a while? It's beautiful today, isn't it." Elizabeth sat down next to her on the steps and peeled off her gloves.

"You'll get your dress dirty sitting out here on the porch," she mumbled. Elizabeth shrugged.

"Since we're neighbors, we should at least know each other's names. Mine's Elizabeth," she said, trying not to stare at her lip. "What's yours?"

"Helen," the woman said. "Helen Owens."

"Are you and your husband from around here?" Elizabeth asked.

Helen shook her head. "We're from Bakersfield. Tommy wanted to move to the city, get away from our families. He thinks he can be in cowboy movies." Helen shook her head again. "That's what he wants, anyway."

"And you? What do you want?" Elizabeth asked.

Helen stared at her. "Who cares what I want," she said. "It doesn't make any difference." She wiped her face and rubbed her bruised arm. She looked at Elizabeth, her eyes blank. "But here's what I wish, what I wish would happen. I wish the baby would sleep at night. Then Tommy won't be so mad at me all the time."

Elizabeth didn't believe that Tommy cared if the baby slept or not. She had several unpleasant encounters with him since she moved in, usually at night when she came home late, and he was outside smoking alone. She didn't think now was the time to share those encounters with Helen. One of the things she had to get used to in her new life were the unwanted advances from men like Tommy. This she despised.

She gently touched Helen's hand. "I hear the way he treats you. I can see it. Why don't you go back home to your family in Bakersfield? It has to be better than this."

Helen jumped up and brushed off her dress. "Why don't you mind your own business," she said. "Do you think I want to talk to you? I don't even know you." She pulled her apartment door open. "What makes you think you know anything about being married anyway?"

Elizabeth grabbed her box and stood up. "Maybe you should ask me some time," she said. "I know enough that I didn't want to be married anymore." She stepped inside her apartment and slipped off her shoes and dress, regretting the encounter with Helen. She would avoid her from now on. Elizabeth laid down on the sofa and closed her eyes.

It was getting dark when she awoke. Elizabeth poured herself a glass of gin, walked outside barefoot and lit a cigarette. She loved Los Angeles at night, the way the jasmine smelled, the city lights, and the moon that hung low on the horizon as evening began. She sat quietly, watching people inside their apartments go about the business of living. It relaxed her, watching the transition between day and night. She took another sip of gin.

She was feeling a little drunk when Tommy burst out of his apartment and strode over to her front steps. She lit another cigarette and looked at his face. At first glance he was handsome, dark with a strong jaw and even features. This illusion was sustained until he opened his mouth. His teeth were short and stained, and there was one tooth missing on the bottom.

"You been talking to my wife today," he said. "Helen's pretty unhappy. She thinks I'm treating her bad."

"You are," Elizabeth said. "I hear you fighting all the time. She's miserable. She sits outside and cries so she doesn't wake up the baby."

"She's my wife," he said. "And what happens in our house isn't anyone's business, including yours. She does what I say too." He grabbed Elizabeth's arm. "Mind your own business from now own. I don't need you giving Helen any of your bullshit ideas." He yanked her arm again, hard.

"Is that gin?" he asked her, looking at her glass. Elizabeth nodded. He smiled at her, his teeth ugly and feral in the dim light. "Get me a drink and maybe I'll forget about you talking to Helen today."

Elizabeth stood up and went into her apartment. He slipped inside behind her and closed the door. She was afraid now. She got a glass and poured him a drink. He drank it in one long gulp and motioned her to pour him another.

"It's hot in here," she said. "Let's go back outside." She tried to slip around him, but his body blocked the door. He pinned her against the wall and kissed her, his tongue hard and slimy in her mouth.

"I'd rather stay here," he said. "We can drink the rest of the bottle." He kissed her again, pinning her arms to keep her from struggling.

"Just a minute, wait a minute," Elizabeth gasped. "I have something you'll like a lot better than drugstore gin." She squirmed out of his arms and grabbed her purse. She felt around until she found the envelope and opened it with shaking fingers. She sprinkled the white powder on the countertop and rolled up one of her new $5.00 bills.

"Sniff some of this," she said. "I know you movie people love heroin." She handed him the rolled-up bill. "Show me how to do it," she said. "I've never tried it before."

He looked confused as he stared at the little pyramid of powder. He ran his finger along the bill. "You know, I've only been in a couple of movies as an extra," he said tentatively. "I'm hoping to get a little stunt work next." He looked at Elizabeth. "I just sniff it through this?" he asked.

She nodded. Beads of sweat ran down her back. "That's what I hear," she said.

Tommy plunged the rolled-up bill into the pile and took a deep inhale. He stumbled back and threw up on the kitchen floor. He ran out her front door and staggered toward his own apartment. Elizabeth watched as he tripped and fell on his front stairs, his head hitting the concrete with a dull thud. His body jerked for a few seconds, and then he was still.

Elizabeth closed her door. She wet a rag under the kitchen faucet and washed the rest of the powder off the counter, then hid the rag and the envelope in the back of her closet. She'd throw it away tomorrow morning, after she figured out what she would say to the police. She sat on her sofa expectantly, wondering what would happen next.

BLUE HOUR

The urge came out of nowhere, and suddenly Lily had to leave. She grabbed her purse, her car keys, a couple of masks, and texted her fiancé. "Can't take it anymore. Be back in a few days. Road trip." Hugh would be pissed off, but not exactly surprised. Lily had been out of sorts for months. She felt spacy and slow, her mind was not working right.

Since the country had gone into full lockdown, Lily hadn't driven her car in months. It was new before the pandemic, when she still cared about things like new cars, new clothes, and Botox. She hopped inside and saw that the gas tank was still full. She had no particular destination in mind except getting out of West Seattle.

Lily's new car was keyless. She fumbled with the fob, trying to remember how to get it started. She stared at the buttons on the dash, and decided to push the big one labeled "Start." It worked. She decided to drive south until she felt like stopping. There were hardly any cars on I5, and Lily could drive as fast as she wanted. It felt good, surreal to have the freeway to herself.

After a couple of hours speeding down the freeway, Lily had to go to the bathroom. She decided she probably needed to get some gas and something to eat before it got dark. She was almost in Portland, Oregon. She had to think a few minutes about what she needed to do. Find a gas station, use the bathroom, grab some Budweiser and Cheetos, and fill up her tank. After she took care of business, Lily decided she'd drive further south. She pulled off the freeway at the downtown exit.

Before the shutdown, Lily was thoroughly sick of Portland. As of a year ago, she had been traveling to Portland a couple of times a month for work. By reflex she drove straight to the Benson Hotel. Broadway was empty, so she parked her new car in front of the revolving entry doors.

Before the first wave of the virus, Lily hated both business travel and the Benson Hotel. During the first lockdown, Lily was thrilled that she no longer had to travel. A silver lining of sorts, although Lily had never been one to look for silver linings in any situation. As far as she was concerned, she'd be happy never to pack her suitcase with Brooks Brothers suits and conservative heels.

Over the last several months of the second lockdown, Lily had drastically changed her mind regarding her former life. All her likes and dislikes were modified in ways she never expected. Staying at a hotel and attending work in person, dressed up in something other than sweatpants, now seemed like a perfect way to spend a couple of days. She looked at the Benson through her car window. No valet, no doorman. She wondered where all those people were now.

She got out of her car, walked up to the revolving door and shoved it a couple of times. It was locked. She read the sign, although she knew what it would say. "Closed Indefinitely for COVID. See You Soon. The Benson." She peered inside. The hotel was empty. A couple of lights were on, so Lily assumed the hotel still had electricity. That meant the elevator might work.

Lily walked around the front of the hotel to the Seventh Avenue alley access door. When her stays were regular, she used to go downstairs and have a cigarette in the rear alley with the hotel staff. After they were done smoking, they would let her inside the hotel through the back entrance, an old metal swing door with a glass window.

Lily looked around the alley to see if anyone was watching her. She heard shouts and laughter of what she assumed were the homeless and mentally ill, but didn't see anyone. She searched the alley, found a brick, and smashed out the glass at the top of the door. It felt satisfying and relaxing. She took her first deep breath of the day and smiled.

Lily stood on her tiptoes, stuck her arm through the hole, and grabbed the door handle. It opened easily from the inside. She stepped into the dark passageway and headed down the hall toward the lobby. Her arm hurt and she felt it dripping. She rubbed her hand on the trickles and licked her fingers. It was blood, probably from the glass. She'd find a towel or something to wrap it once she got to a bathroom.

Lily ran her hand down the hallway wall until she reached the grand entrance lobby. It was dusty and dark. The air smelled stale. Lily stood still, trying to blink the dust out of her eyes. The Benson was completely silent. She could hear herself breathe. She was surprised the lobby wasn't pitch black. Instead it was several shades of blue; deep dark tones. Silvery-blue dust motes floated in the air. As her eyes adjusted to the dim light, the lobby gradually became visible.

The Benson had always given her the creeps, which was a large part of its appeal. The hotel was old, on Portland's historic register. The grand lobby and staircase remained intact, with polished brown wainscot, inlaid parquet floors, and plaster moldings on the ceiling. It was a Gilded Age masterpiece of architectural details. When Lily stayed there, she felt the energy of the past, all the people who stayed there before. Some good vibes, some bad vibes. Maybe some ghosts.

There were newer, nicer hotels in Portland, but she always stayed at the Benson. She hated and loved it at the same time. The biggest complaint modern guests had about the Benson was coincidentally the same thing she liked best about it. The rooms were tiny. She felt secure when she stayed there, the small rooms were all decorated with the same faded striped wallpaper and dusty velvet curtains with gold corded pulls. Plus, it was easy to walk from the bed to the bathroom in the middle of the night.

She turned on her phone's flashlight and made her way to the long mahogany bar. She grabbed a half-empty bottle of bourbon and a glass and headed to the elevators. Her hand shook as she pushed the UP button. The light went on. She heard the elevator groan, cables whining as it headed to the lobby. The doors slowly creaked open. She got in, and hit the button for the 12th floor.

Lily always stayed in the same room at the Benson, Room 1215. The staff would save it for her when she made a reservation. It was a quiet corner room, away from the ice machine and the elevator, and Lily didn't feel like it was haunted. She felt some weird vibes, but nothing that really scared her.

She established travel rituals to enforce some sort of familiarity. After she checked in, she headed straight to her room and unpacked her luggage. After hanging up her clothes, Lily would pour herself a drink from the minibar. After a couple of sips, she would push the heavy velvet curtains open and watch the city lights until the sun went down. The windows in the room were operable; she could open the biggest one and lean out onto the wide windowsill ledge. She tried not to look to the right.

Lily always assumed Room 1215 did not have a ghost because of the massive iron gargoyle perched on the corner building ledge next to the window. She would avert her eyes as she leaned out on the ledge, not wanting to look at his scowling metal face and hunched iron back. She would make sure to close the curtains at night so she couldn't see his shadow reflected on the hotel floor.

The door to Room 1215 was locked. Lily set down her purse and the bottle of bourbon, and began kicking the doorknob steadily, patiently, and persistently until the lock broke and the door swung open. She threw her purse and the bottle on the bed, and immediately went to the tiny bathroom. There was no toilet paper, but the Kleenex box was full. She slowly ran her hand along the wall until she felt a light switch.

Lily turned on the light and immediately flicked it back off. Cockroaches scattered into all four corners.

The bed, end tables, curtains and chairs were caked with a thick oily dust. In the semi-darkness, the room returned to soothing shades of blue. She took a deep breath, the second deep breath of the day. It made her light-headed, dizzy. The musty smell in the room overwhelmed her.

She poured herself a drink, walked over to the big window and opened it to get some fresh air. She leaned out onto the ledge and took another deep breath. Lily couldn't stop herself from looking at the gargoyle. He was as ugly as she remembered, now spattered with bird shit. The gargoyle's face was a grinning metal rictus, his teeth jagged, his bulging eyes eternally opened wide.

The stale air and whiskey made Lily feel faint. She pushed the window open wider, set her drink down, and climbed out onto the ledge. Since she was alone in the hotel, Lily decided it was finally her chance to smoke a cigarette in her room. Pandemic benefits. She fished one out of a half-empty pack, lit it and took a deep inhale.

The gargoyle blinked, and turned his head toward her with a metallic grinding creak. Lily screamed and dropped her cigarette. Everyone she knew referred to the ongoing pandemic situation as "the new normal." Lily preferred to characterize it as it really was —a waking nightmare. She assumed the now-animate gargoyle was yet another horrible side effect of COVID.

The gargoyle flexed his wings and scratched his feet with his long pointy nails as Lily stared. She finished her drink, and lit another cigarette. Lung cancer was the least of her concerns anymore.

"You're back," the gargoyle said. His voice was harsh and grating, like worn-out brake pads. "I haven't seen you or anyone else up here for a long time." He stretched his long arms and motioned to the empty city below. "What's going on down there?"

"I don't know," Lily said. "Everyone's sick, getting over being sick, getting sick again, or they're dead. Nobody really knows what's happening anymore." She looked at him curiously. "How long have you been here?" she asked.

His face contorted, and he began making sharp grinding sounds. Lily hoped he was laughing. "I've sat up here since 1912," he said. "I've seen so many of you come and go. You've had horses, you've had cars, and your clothes are always strange." He blinked his metal eyes a couple of times, click-click. "I just sit and watch you humans stumble through your short lives day after day after day, making a mess out of everything."

Lily stubbed her cigarette out on the ledge and threw it into the street below. She stared into night sky in silence. She didn't know if she was awake or dreaming anymore. To be honest, she had stopped caring a couple of months ago. The stars were bright, and the night sky was a soft deep blue.

She sat quietly as the gargoyle stood up, watching him pace back and forth on the ledge while flapping his iron wings. They clanged and clattered. "You're loud," she said. "I'm used to it being quiet now." Lily used to hate traffic noise, loud talking, airplane noise, people chewing with their mouths open, and garbage trucks slamming dumpsters around at 5 in the morning. It was finally quiet, but Lily feared this new silence.

Lily's head began to ache. She poured herself another drink, drained her glass, and tossed it off the ledge. They both watched it fall and shatter on the ground below. She was tired.

"Are you ready now?" the gargoyle asked, holding out his hand. "Let me get my phone first," she said. "You don't need your phone anymore," he said. Lily grabbed his cold hand, and slowly pulled herself up to standing on the ledge. She looked down at the empty city below her, then steadied herself and stared up at the night sky.

She looked at the gargoyle and nodded. "I'm ready now," she said. "Let's go."

ELAINE BONOW

Elaine Bonow is a woman running full speed ahead. Primarily I teach adult ballet classes and old school conditioning for the people.

All of my icons are dead—my mother Laurie Gunter, my ballet teacher Irene Larsson, and my flute teacher Ronnie Pierce.

When I returned to the UW after a lifetime, I finally got a BA in English Literature around 2005.

Simultaneously I started playing a Stratocaster and singing in my band Stupid Boy. After that, I started singing jazz standards while learning to play the flute. Not done yet, I am attempting to play the piano and understand music theory. Never a dull moment.

My daughter and I operate our very eclectic boutique called Ola Wyola.

Catch me if you can. I still have a bunch to do in the next twenty or so years.

DEEP WINTER LIGHT

"Hi; thanks for taking me seriously. My name is Lois and you must be Miss…"

"Just call me Judith, and I will call you Lois if that is alright with you?"

"Yes fine, that will be fine; so. Judith, if you don't mind, let's go upstairs to the sun porch. I enjoy sitting there more and more since I'm older; and especially this time of the year, after the leaves have disappeared from the trees and their black branches can't even cast a shadow in this flat grey light."

The two ladies went up the stairs and towards the front of the house. There, beyond the French doors. was a narrow room encased by windows on three sides. Lois chattered, a little breathlessly, without stopping.

"I have lived here for fifty years, actually fifty-five years in January. My neighborhood is a very pleasant urban suburb, you know what I mean; mostly well-built houses with a few modern houses replacing the ones that were rentals."

She motioned for me to sit at a table covered by a white table-cloth, fifties style adorned with red apples and cherries.

"The strange house I am concerned with is a house up the street, actually across the street, that was a rental until about six months ago when it sold in what seemed like a day. I thought we could have some tea," Lois added.

She had an electric kettle and an old fashioned, British-type teapot and cups with matching saucers, along with a plate of Pepperidge Farm cookies. I was late getting there. It was a little after three.

"It's almost three, you must be starved," Lois said; "well, if you aren't, I sure am. Help yourself. I am so happy to have some company especially in winter. At least I have this sun porch. I feel that I can keep in touch with the world from my perch up here on the porch." She laughed at the turn of phrase, gobbled a Milano double-dark cookie and poured herself another cup of tea.

She brought her face closer to mine. Her glasses were smeary and there were a few cookie crumbs around her mouth.

"Well Judith, you see, I can see that house, especially now that there are no leaves, so easily from my perch. See, it's like this. The other night, well it wasn't so much night as dark, and I do mind my own business but this was so unusual for the neighborhood. I mean I was out here on the sun porch just getting up to go to the bathroom, and I noticed a series of lights blinking—no, not blinking, but two flashes followed by three flashes, and that kept repeating; but when I got back from the bathroom they had stopped. And I didn't think anything about it.

"But then the next night, the same time, the same thing. So I decided that this needed some investigation. I tried to find my binoculars to see what was going on up close but I never found them. Someone must have borrowed them but I thought if I looked carefully I might be able to figure out what was going on. I even took a casual stroll around past the house. From the outside it looked exactly the same way it had before it was sold. Nothing was different. Same curtains. Closed. No one had lived there for almost a year.

"I decided that this time I would turn off all the lights up here on the sun porch so I could see better and I thought that right before the usual time for the light show I saw a man in a white shirt carrying something, came out of the front door and seemed to get in a car parked out front. The lights did their dance and finally stopped. "Wait, I'm glad you got here late; you can see what I mean."

It was dark already when she told me this. I didn't know exactly why she had called; but I am always prepared for the unknown, and happened to have a high-powered pair of night vision binoculars in my purse. She was delighted seeing these when I showed them to her. I told her I was prepared to wait until the light show.

She went downstairs and returned with a tray of sandwiches and a pot of coffee. We took turns in the bathroom and settled into the darkness of the sun porch. It was warm in the narrow room and I fought drowsiness after the sandwich and the coffee affected me like a sleeping pill.

It was about one a.m. when she stood up. She whispered, "wake up Judith, wake up." I grabbed the binoculars and adjusted them for the night vision. It was easy for me to see the details around the house and see where the lights were coming from. I saw a man open the front door, shut the door, open and shut again, like he had forgotten something.

He went to the car, opening and closing it three times. He repeated his actions at least four times finally getting in his car.

He drove off. I stayed at my post and was rewarded ten minuets later when the man returned to his parking place.

"Lois, I think I understand what is happening. Your neighbor has OCD. Obsessive compulsive disorder; he's not a murderer or a thief, he is just a little nuts. But I'm glad we police could be here to help you sleep better."

SOUP

"What's for lunch?"

"Soup today as usual; it's Wednesday after all."

"OK, I'll be there around eleven."

It was one of the last days of summer. Nightfall was earlier and earlier. She harvested the last of the heirloom tomatoes, their color much less vibrant than even two weeks ago.

Two of these fat beauties were on their way to the soup pot. She always made soup on Wednesdays, which she took to the local shelter. Living in a small town had its bonuses; and this one, being able to share her cooking with friends, was a highlight. She gathered all the odds and ends of vegetables she had saved during the week and that others had donated to her cause: zucchini, potatoes, cabbages, a garlic, onions; you name it, someone was growing it for the soup.

It was only recently however, that he became a regular Wednesday afternoon visitor to her home. He was younger than her, but somehow, so far they fit. She finished making the soup turning it down low to gently meld the vegetables and herbs into a delightful brew, and made a cup of tea. Melda took the tea out to her favorite spot, where the weak sun shone from mid-morning on the east-facing porch.

She had lived here now for just about five years; finally escaping the city, exchanging that life for a slice of nature on the glorious peninsula. At first she was lonely and a bit discouraged, but soon adjusted to the pace and found some friends and a sense of value in the community.

When the sun turned the corner she knew it was time to check the soup; plus he would be getting here soon. She took a little bowl from the cabinet, and grabbed a spoon. Tasting in her opinion was an art form. Knowing exactly what was lacking in flavor is what the Japanese call umami, that flavor that makes you smack your lips in delight. You also need an eye for beauty, a nose as sensitive as a hound, and a genuine love of food.

After her taste, she quickly corrected the saltiness; another taste, she put in olive oil and gave it a stir. The pepper grinder was turned exactly fifteen turns; and she turned the burner off. "Almost there," she said after another few spoonfuls.

Melda hurried to her small bedroom and changed, because he was coming over. She was a casual woman, and usually wore comfortable pants and long-sleeved tops. Today, however, she took a little more time. She had a new pink sweater that was waiting for an autumnal afternoon; plus people said she looked good in pink whenever she wore it.

"I do have some jeans here somewhere?" she said. "They will look much better than these old pants." Usually around the house she never bothered with a bra, but today she didn't want her nipples to show against the lightweight pink sweater.

She looked in the bathroom mirror and said aloud, "I'm glad make-up isn't needed here." It seemed as if no one on this ancient coast ever wore make-up except shop ladies and shopkeepers. Melda brushed her teeth, put a little natural cream on her face and a dab of her personal mix of essential oils and went out into the back garden.

James was looking forward to Melda's soup. He drove his truck northward until he was at the top of the hill overlooking the city. This area of town was like a little town in a little town. They had a country store instead of a chain supermarket. There was a breakfast restaurant owned and operated by the same family for over fifty years now. The most important business was the neighborhood center. That's where he first heard of Melda's soup after getting a bowl and being really impressed.

He helped out at the center when something needed fixing and of course would trade his labors for food. James had been in town for almost a year and lived on the top of the hill actually just a few blocks from Melda.

He dashed into his apartment, a converted motel from the fifties with two stories and no kitchens in the rooms to speak of, just a hot plate and a tiny refrigerator. There was still a pay for ice machine at the back of the stairwell.

The Sound View Motel was not glamorous but cheap, and everyone minded their own business.

It was already after eleven when he headed down and around the corner to Melda's, parked, and found her in the garden. She didn't see him at first, busy digging some weeds from the soil. He spotted her soft mane of hair and then her face. He noticed that the color pink suited her dark complexion. He was pleased that she didn't have on make-up. His ex-partner was so narcissistic and one of the reasons why he left the city because he felt that life must have more to offer for him. He didn't feel right until he let go and changed. Just like that. He changed and for the first time in a while he felt a little bit better about life.

"Hey, Miss Melda, it's me, James."

She looked up, took off her gloves, and shaded her eyes above her shades.

"Oh James, is it one o'clock already?" she said, a big smile growing across her face.

"Sorry; I'm a little late but I'm ready for some soup." He walked across the small space to the edge of the garden.

Standing next to him felt good. He wasn't a pretty man unless you saw him from some weird light. Otherwise, in other lights, he could look almost classically ugly. He was thin and bald; gangly but with a nice shaped head. He a tall man just about six feet she thought.

"Well, you are just in time. The soup has to re-heat for about twelve minutes first. I made some tea. No wait; let's have some coffee." She reached up to get the Moka coffee pot, filled it with water and coffee, and put it on the burner.

James took off his hat and said, "What can I do? I am a helpful person. I actually like to help."

"Ah; well then, just take the bread and cut a few slices. We'll eat this on the porch today."

James did as he was told and found that being near her in that tiny kitchen aroused him. The soup smelled good and he was hungry. She had to brush by him to get some butter and jam. He didn't move. He could smell her though, and he almost jumped out of the kitchen to the porch and sat down. Melda brought out a small tureen of the soup. They sipped the coffee, waiting for the soup to cool down. They buttered bread and dipped it in the soup. James didn't know how to begin. Melda was thrilled to be so obviously courted. She thought that they should probably try to become friends before stepping off the deep end.

Both were old enough to realize the consequences of teenage

behavior, but it was too late. Melda suggested that they have a spot of brandy with another cup of coffee. They somehow ended up together in that small kitchen. He thought he would let her make the first move so he wouldn't seem too much like a "horn-dog," but they both magnetized against the corner cabinets. He pressed his body to hers and she yielded.

DEATH OF THE SUN

So many things happened at the end of the decade, so many strange things that to explain it all I have to go back to the beginning.

I always consult my horoscope every morning and this particular morning was no exception. Plus I write down my dreams and get an interpretation from my favorite Internet site. After that, I throw down a Celtic Cross Tarot reading for myself and all this is before my cup of green tea (matcha for you uninitiated), and I've already given my room a quick smudgy sage.

You might ask how long this ritual awakening takes, but I've always been a light sleeper and an early riser. Of course, that magic hour, 4:44, the time when angels are most active, is my best time to wake up. Don't get me wrong; I'm no angel by any means because I do take a re-nap from six till nine, so you see I'm not that strange.

But getting back to the weird events that happened on the solstice, the winter solstice, not the equinox. I always get the two confused, which is comical since I am such the occult freak.

Every solstice should be celebrated as a very festive occurrence with parties, parades, a homage to life; especially the winter solstice, which now days is just one of the final shopping days before the Holy Day of Spending known as Christmas. However, this day the solstice was on a Saturday and I had a busy schedule.

Oh yeah, first things first. Lately my dreams involved being at a party with hundreds of people—parties in a park, parties at a house, parties in a club.

Of course, I've looked up the meaning of being in a large crowd on my favorite Internet page about the meaning of dreams, auntieflo.com. All of my crowd dreams are happy and full of fun and this is only interpreted as a positive dream and another page suggests that I have "a strong support system."

Nothing really interesting or profound here so I figure it must be just a dream about me having a good time in my dreams, especially since I don't have any social anxiety and I'm not naked. So let me move on to the horoscope.

I use another Internet page for my own personal daily horoscope; but today it was rather bland, just like my dream and not even worth writing down. Sometimes I do wonder if all this interpretation of my so-called subconscious is worth all the time and effort; but since I am trying to be a more enlightened soul, I guess I have to keep up this façade of worthiness.

A little discouraged (this was, after all, supposed to be an auspicious day), I decided to skip the whole (most of the time un-decipherable) Celtic Cross Tarot reading and just pick one card. I casually shuffled the deck, and, not at all like I usually do, turned over the first card, great the Ten of Pentacles, the money card; good fortune for me today.

This made me feel a whole lot better for the day ahead. I had to finish my yule preparations for the next day; plus, I was excited to go to the solstice party tonight. The Death of the Sun was at precisely 8:19 west coast time.

I had already collected and hung the greenery, holly, mistletoe, and lots of cedar swag around my place. My donation to the party was to bring more greenery, so we could all make a gigantic yule log to be lit on fire at the exact moment, that being 8:19 here and at Stonehenge.

This was a first for me, since I had only joined this pagan group earlier this year on the summer solstice, from a meetup I found on the Internet.

Finally everything was ready. I had on my yule colors: red, green and white. When I looked in the mirror however, I thought I resembled Mrs. Claus, and that made me feel just a little stupid. After all, I am not that old, not even close; and I really wanted to get some attention, especially from the big Kahuna, Bobby K. We all just use our first names and one last initial to be anonymous in the world of the Internet.

I mean, Bobby K was so charismatic. He was the chief druid of the group. He was tall and well built and, even stranger for a druid, he was a Black man with an enormous tangle of dreads.

At our meetings he would strip down to his old school basketball shorts and lead the drum circle. All of us, men and women, would become totally enthralled by his, well, by his everything.

He claimed to be descended from his Celtic druid mother who was born in Wales and his Nigerian Yoruba father whose lineage is all spiritual and shit.

I changed my clothes to become a sexy witch with some cleavage, and let my hair out of its usual ponytail. My usual pinkish lipstick I replaced with some Revlon really red, red lips. I clipped some mistletoe in my hair with some glittery clips someone gave me last Christmas.

I re-checked myself in the mirror and was pleasantly surprised by my transformation. "Watch out Mr. Bobby K, this witch is ready for a Soulful solstice."

Gah, it was already a little after 7:00 by the time I found the place. It was out on the Eastside, in the woods in an old lodge that belonged to one of the members of the pagan tribe. I didn't expect to see so many people, but this end of the decade solstice brought out people from miles away. It was a bit chilly but no rain in sight. We might even be able to see the waning crescent moon if we were still up at dawn.

I went inside the lodge and immediately was handed a wassail cup. I dragged my big bag of mistletoe and holly to a corner and started handing out my bundles to people as they streamed by. Everyone was dressed in green, red, and white. The music started with a live rock band.

There were paintings on all the walls. Some were, to my absolute surprise, erotic—and a few absolutely pornographic. I overheard a couple of men talking. "It's a great piece of art, it's just not something anyone wants to buy."

"Oh yes, I agree; that is, unless you had a secret room in your house and could hide it there," the other man said with a chuckle.

Since I was there by myself, and only knew a few faces from our meetups, I decided to keep circling the vast room. I went upstairs to check out the bathrooms and I had to pee when I overheard two women in one of the stalls talking.

They sounded like they were sniffing some cocaine when one said, "See, the story starts like this—Two puppets meet in a grocery store and…"

"What kind of puppets?"

"Clown puppets, silly."

"What do these clown puppets do for a living?"

"I think they are working in a circus."

"Oh yeah, that makes sense."

Dang, I thought, that doesn't make any sense. Why would puppets be shopping in a grocery store in the first place? Well, that thought cracked me up; and before they figured out that I was spying on them, I flushed and ran out without washing my hands, oh well.

When I went downstairs, I saw everyone leaving out the back. I followed the crowd, which was getting pretty tipsy and high, to the circle set up around a huge pile of wood.

On top of the pyre was a Christmas tree with ornaments and tinsel and cranberry and popcorn wreaths, angel on top and everything. Gorgeous!

I looked at my phone it was already 8:15. I took a selfie with the pyre in the background. Everyone was doing the same. Someone gave me another cup of wassail. It was much stronger than the first. I was already feeling different a bit altered.

The time inched closer. Bobby K appeared in a white robe. He was holding a huge torch made of sticks and straw. The crowd started chanting while the band droned. I could just make out,

"...Fresh and clean... in time and space... as the sun returns... so shall it be."

And WOOSH, Bobby K tossed the burning torch into the pyre, which caught in an instant. The crowd went wild, bursting into song and dance. I could see their mouths wide open by the firelight. The decorated Christmas tree caught fire. That was right before the baby flew into the air and into the flames. The crowd was silenced and then let out a cheer—"The sun is dead, long live the sun."

I was stunned. I was shocked and then I realized that this was no real baby. It was an effigy of Jesus the Son, a pagan homage to the rebirth of the sun.

I wasn't aware that I had fainted until I was being resuscitated by Bobby K blowing his breath into my mouth.

THAT'LL TEACH YOU

Jordy. How can you trust a person named Jordy? I don't understand why my sister was even attracted to him much less think of marrying Jordy AKA Jordan Sparks. The thing I hated the most about him wasn't just his stupid nickname, Jordy, it was his pathetic abuse of my sisters' innocence and gullibility.

She met him at her BFF's bachelorette party in Vegas last summer.

"Albert darling, can you believe it. I met the man I'm going to marry."

"Hold on sis." I said, "You just met this joker and he wants to marry you already? Are you nuts?" I was almost screaming into the phone. Judy started sobbing on the other end.

"Jesus, I'm sorry sis; I didn't mean to make you cry. It's just not a good sign when someone you hardly know wants to get married right away. That's a typical move for a stone cold narcissist. I thought you took psychology 101 in college."

The thing is this: Judy, being my only sister, has always been a lonely girl and very shy. I feel that I have to protect her, especially since our mother's death. Mom was so careful with the both of us. We were just kids when our dad died. We became her responsibility. When she died she left us very well off, a legacy of her father and his father before him.

Sure, you could say I was over-protective of Judy, but I loved my little sister. We've always been close, barely a year apart. All of my pleading had no effect. I couldn't stop her.

"Al, just wait until you meet Jordy. You two are so much alike. I just know you two will be best friends. I just know it."

But when I met Jordy I hated him at first sight. You've heard about love at first sight; well, this was the total opposite. There was something pedestrian in his manner. The way he walked towards me his thick blunt hand extended.

Everything about him was blunt; those thick khaki clad legs, short thick feet in hiking boots for Christ's sake, a blue denim shirt, topped off by a ridiculous outback type of hat. He shook my hand pumping away effusively; and, after a god-awful "bro" chest bump, he swept off those tinted aviator glasses and prattled, "So glad to meet you, Albert, I've heard so much about you."

Judy looked happy. In fact, it was the first time I'd seen her laughing and smiling since, well, since way before Mom died. Judy spent years taking care of mom. She'd drive her to doctor's appointments, to physical therapy, wheeling her up the avenue to do shopping or have tea with her old lady friends. She did this without too much complaint, at least not to me. She hardly went out even with friends, keeping house, doing the cooking, laundry, and cleaning.

Together, they indulged in movies from the video store and wearing out Redbox rentals; but by the time the phenomenon known as Netflix came along, our mom had died. That was how they lived for years. I felt guilty, having a lived life of my own; and I was thankful that Judy sacrificed her life to take care of mom. And now there was this Jordy.

He moved right into her apartment. They had his life shipped in from California. It was not a light load. He was here to stay. Cars, a huge pick-up truck, a couple of motorcycles, cheap furniture, and what must have been a month's worth of matching khaki pants and blue denim shirts. What I didn't see moving in was a very substantial booze and drug habit.

At first he just seemed to drink—a lot. I know I drink, but I didn't drink like he did. Judy tried to keep up with him, but my once-sheltered angel of mercy was in danger of sliding into a cheap floozy, right before my eyes.

They had a favorite bar that they frequented, just a couple of blocks away from the apartment.

"Al, we aren't hurting anyone. We never drive and drink. It's just so much fun." Judy explained this new life story to me when I happened to drop by one afternoon. I couldn't deny her having fun after so much she had given to mom.

"Oh, and Jordy says you should call first before you come over. You know, we might be cuddling and not want to be disturbed, OK." And she kissed me away.

I tried calling a couple of times but no one would answer the phone—ever. The voice message was turned off and there was no way to reach Judy by email. That is until one night I got a call from Judy.

"Al, Al, I don't know what's happening. Jordy left this afternoon and he hasn't been back. This has never happened before and I don't know what to do."

"Shhh, don't cry now. Tell me what happened."

"Well, we, I mean I was asleep and heard the front door slam. No first the phone rang. He got up, went out of the room and then he was gone. I waited and waited. I got so freaked out so I took a couple more Xanax…"

"When did you start taking those?"

"Oh for a while now. Jordy thought I could use some and Dr. Adams gave me a prescription for my nerves. And also some Percocets for the pain I have in my back."

"I didn't know you had a pain condition. Why didn't you tell me?"

"Oh wait, hold on, I hear the door. I'd better hang up. Jordy, Jordy is that you?"

I heard him in the distance. "Judy what the fuck, get up. Let's go get some cash. Who are you talki…"?

He called me right back. "Listen Al, you goddamn faggot. Don't call here again, ya hear me."

I was about to say. "Hell Jordy, I didn't call; Judy called me." I was pissed. Who the hell did he think he was, calling me names? This was a wake-up call, and my first indication that something was terribly wrong.

I was able to convince our bank to show me Judy's withdrawals. I was stunned. In the six months since Jordy's arrival, sixty thousand dollars had been taken out in cash. I had to do something and do something quick. I didn't want to hurt Judy but this predator had to be stopped.

And I knew just how to do it. My plan took a couple of weeks to set up. He never knew what hit him. I was able to capture him after setting him up with an old dope dealer friend of mine who easily found out what kind of drugs Jordy was spending the money on. I realize that it sounds very melodramatic; but when you have money like I do, you can afford the drama.

One of my newly-formed gang, well paid by me, had buddied up to him in the bar. "We" slipped a couple of roofies in his beer and hustled him outside on the pretense of selling him some really good Peruvian cocaine. He fell hook, line, and sinker. It was brilliant. The cocaine was heroin. He went out like a light; not enough to kill him, mind you, just put him into a druggie coma.

We put him in the back seat of the SUV. I drove all night, stopping after eight hours for a couple of hours sleep. The last few hours would be off road. I knew the way, although it had been a few years since I'd been to the old cabin.

He was still asleep when I arrived. It was a beautiful place high in the north Idaho mountains. I left him with a couple of weeks' supply of water and food. There was plenty of firewood, blankets, and warm clothing.

By the time he sobers up and figures that if he wants to leave, he'll have to walk out. He'll learn that playing dirty with my little family can be dangerous to assholes like him. I did leave him a note: "Jordy, when you do decide to walk out, be sure to watch out for bears."

MAGICAL THINKING

"Yeah, let me tell you it was only a dream but it was so fucking real." Fread shouted at Larry as they walked back to the tavern.

"But just why are you so freaked out about it. Dreams are just a rehash of what happens to us during the day or the past few days. I mean that's what I've been told. Really now, there is no reason to believe all this will happen just cause you dreamed it."

"You are just a non-believer in psychic truth. I only told you because I thought you were my friend and you of all people wouldn't dis me."

"I'm still pissed. That was our last conversation." Larry took a long swallow of his beer and then threw down a shot of Jamison's.

"But he's your best friend," Sandy said. "You guys are tight like real brothers. Y'all have so much time and history together.

"Sure, you're right about that. We have been buds since right after college really, and after we just drifted around." Larry smiled as the memories flashed through his mind. "I remember those days and sometimes I wish we were still there—the time before we had to be people really. You know, I mean grown-up people."

"Right on, I remember when we could just wander here and there. Work when we needed money and then drift. I could sleep on your couch."

"And then I could sleep on yours." They laughed at the thoughts of the good old days.

"We were free, no ties, no responsibilities. What the fuck happened?"

"Hell, we became real people with shit to do." Sandy and Larry went out to the alley behind the tavern to smoke a pre-rolled joint. The air was quiet and warm.

"Well I have more shit to do than be freaked out by Fread fucking Gardner."

"Do you think he is just tripping or is he on something?"

"You mean something more that cannabis, vodka, internet sex, various pills and what about that chick he is screwing... What's her name?"

"Oh you mean Joey—Joey who was a dude then became a chick and then became a chick with a dick? That Joey?"

"Oh shit, I forgot about that."

"Freaddy is actually a very enlightened soul."

"How's that?" Sandy said lighting his bong. "How's that? He mumbled again in that voice people get when they are toking on a hit.

"That's the reason we are still friends. I respect his fucking mind. He has tripped on everything and written about it, at least I read the stuff he wrote and it was deep shit. So when he tells me about that dream, that freaked me out."

Larry and Sandy went back inside the tavern and settled in their favorite back booth. The tavern was empty as usual; only Mike the owner, barkeep, janitor and short-order cook was there behind the bar in his usual corner watching TV on his computer.

Larry leaned back; quiet now that he was stoned. The weed hit his brain and expanded. He let his thoughts wander into those familiar nooks and crannies of stoner thoughts and feelings. Tinged with images, colors, and insights, he let all of this flow until he could come out the other side.

Fread, on his return to his room, closed the curtains, locked his door in order to re-think the dream. He knew that most dreams were just a re-viewing of the episodes in the recent past, a way to make your subconscious work out what had happened and some-how could if you were aware, give you some prediction of your future actions. After all, we all lived on a continuous time–life trajectory. And that, as the ancient adage teaches us, is that every action has a reaction; in other words, karma.

But just what the hell did karma have to do with this dream? He had actually been on a substance fast for the past ten days, eating strictly vegan with no drugs or alcohol. He had stayed in his room contemplating finishing the novel he was working on.

Fread wanted to capture the dream in writing. He sat at his desk, grabbed a stack of plain white paper and clicked some more lead in one of the mechanical pencils within reach.

It was a time from the past, sometime in the dark ages where reality and mythology were all mixed up. In the dream a man appeared in swirling velvet robes. The robe opened and the man was naked. The robe fell to the ground; Fread could see that the man's body was covered in tattooed symbols. As he was turning he threw something to Fread.

That vision faded to black; and he was kneeling in front of a woman dressed as a queen, a queen covered in gold. Suddenly he looked up and the woman was now in a kitchen, cooking huge pots of steaming foods. He felt that this woman was his mother but not at all like what his mother had been.

Fread's mother was someone he hadn't talked to for at least two years. He wondered what his mother was doing and thought he might as well call her.

The dream was still on his mind. He kept flashing back to gold, spells, occult symbols, and strange smells. He thought about the object the magician threw to him but couldn't quite see what it was. He remembered what he had told Larry about his dream that it wasn't so much about the dream but about how real it seemed to him, a feeling he hadn't been able to shake all day.

He opened his phone and dialed his mother's number. While the phone rang he felt sad and tears rolled down his face. He hadn't been in touch with her for at least… "Hello, hello?"

There was no one on the line, although someone seems to have answered. Fread hung up the phone and found himself dialing again. This time, a strange voice answered "Hello, hello who is this please?'

"It's me, Fredrick; is my mother there? Who is this?"

"Oh Fredrick, I'm so glad you called. It's your aunt Carmena. I have some bad news. I'm sorry to tell you that your mother has died. In fact she just died last night. She wanted to see you. She wanted to call you but was too sick. It was sudden. She left a letter here for you. Do you want me to read it to you?"

Fread felt as if all the air had been sucked out of his body. When he was able to take a breath, he sat back in his chair and switched on the table lamp. The room was bathed in a golden light. It reminded him of being in the dream. "Yes, please, read it to me."

"Dearest Fredrick, I hope life finds you healthy and surrounded by happiness and light. A lot has happened since I last talked to you. The man you met, Al, the one with all the tattoos, died last spring. I wanted to find you, but I know you wanted to be away from your past and to succeed in pursuing your writing career. I'm sorry we never, or should I say I never, had enough money to provide for you; and of course there was the problem of my mental health, which was so depressing for us both.

"In the past couple of years being in the care of Al I have found salvation; no, not in a conventional way, but in a way that saved me. As a way of repairing my life, and your life and thanks to the generosity of Al, I am leaving you a legacy in gold. Trust me and I trust you to do what is best. Take care of your Aunt Carma and remember to share the wealth and give to the needy, but don't give so much and ruin yourself."

When Fread hung up the phone he looked down on his desk and there in front of him was a gold cross with a tattooed corpus—the very thing the man had thrown to him in the dream.

REN FELMAN

Ren Felman runs a tech consultancy by day and by night writes prose about family drama, teenage adventure, and retiree romance, sometimes in dystopian settings and sometimes not. She also likes to compose silly songs for her two small children. When she grows up she hopes to be a trapeze artist or an astronaut, and if you ask her where she's from she'll tell you: "Far away from here!"

SCREENPLAY:
LOVE IN THE TIME OF CORONAVIRUS

LOGLINE WITH SHOT HEADINGS

It is early March, 2020. With the backdrop of a global pandemic, a brother and sister arrange for the lover of their aging mother to shelter with her and their father, and then move into the family house themselves. Will their mother finally be content and stay home now that all of her loved ones are under one roof?

ACT ONE

The setting is a house in a French suburb. SYLVIE, an attractive 70-year-old woman is preparing to leave for work and her adult son, JULIEN, is trying to convince her not to go.

INT. - SYLVIE & HUBERT'S HOUSE - FOYER (MORNING)

SYLVIE
"But what can I do? It is my job. You worry far too much."

JULIEN grimaces as his mother arranges the foulard around her neck and checks her hair in the hallway mirror.

SYLVIE
"À bientôt, mon amour. I return at 6:00. Make sure Papa has his medicine with lunch."

SYLVIE kisses her son on both cheeks and heads out the door.

EXT. - SYLVIE & HUBERT'S HOUSE—FRONT PATH TO SIDEWALK

SYLVIE winks at JULIEN, who can't help but smile a little, but the smile fades as she click-click-clicks down the street toward the bus stop.

INT. - SYLVIE & HUBERT'S HOUSE - FOYER / NATHALIE'S APARTMENT

JULIEN calls his sister, NATHALIE, to enlist her assistance.

JULIEN
"Nathalie, she's gone in again today."

NATHALIE
"Who? Gone where?"

JULIEN
"Maman! To work! What do you think I'm talking about?"

NATHALIE
"Well, of course she's gone in. What? You think she'll abandon Monsieur Bloch now? Because of a little virus?"

JULIEN
"Monsieur Bloch can take care of himself, no? And it's not a little virus, Nathalie! Be reasonable, please. And at Maman's age, it's so dangerous for her, traipsing around town, probably contracting COVID this moment!"

NATHALIE
"I'm not sure it's that dangerous, Julien. Get a hold of yourself."

JULIEN
"You're wrong, Nathalie. It is extremely dangerous for old people. For Maman, for Papa, for Monsieur Bloch. Fatality rate at 10 percent or something extremely high for those who are older and get infected. If Maman goes out and gets it, she brings it home to Papa who is only here, minding his own business."

NATHALIE
"And maybe she brings it to Monsieur Bloch, too. Yes, that is serious."

JULIEN
"When I saw Nicolas last night..."

NATHALIE
"Oh! Is it back on with Nicolas then? Good for you!"

JULIEN
"Nathalie! What I was starting to say before you so rudely interrupted is that...when I saw Nicolas—just casually, by the way—he said that his boss at the Health Ministry told him that quarantine is coming. He said the order to shut down schools is already drafted."

NATHALIE
"What? I heard that it's gotten bad in Italy but, surely, it won't be like that here... Nicolas, you don't really think it will, do you? If Lilou can't go to school, how will I work?"

JULIEN
"You won't be able to work, Nathalie, and neither will Maman."

NATHALIE
"Oh, Julien. I hardly think we need to still call what Maman does with Monsieur Bloch 'work'."

JULIEN's cheeks flush.

NATHALIE
"Julien? Are you there."

JULIEN
"Yes, I'm here. You don't need to be disrespectful."

NATHALIE
"Listen, if this is really a pandemic and we're really going to be shut inside our houses, Lilou and I are going to come stay with you and Maman and Papa. I don't want to get stuck in our tiny apartment in the city with just the two of us."

JULIEN
"Yes, that seems prudent."

NATHALIE
"And we need to figure out what to do about Monsieur Bloch."

JULIEN
"Why is Monsieur Bloch our responsibility? Surely he has a housekeeper or something?"

NATHALIE
"Maman is not going to give up seeing him. And he is sort of her responsibility... our responsibility. It's been 30 years, Nicolas! He's practically our family."

JULIEN
"Speak for yourself."

Silence.

JULIEN
"But I suppose you're right. Maman won't give him up."

NATHALIE
"And surely Papa can be rational about the situation. Considering the circumstances."

JULIEN whistles.

NATHALIE
"Lilou and I can sleep in the attic room and Monsieur Bloch can have my old room. And Maman can sleep where she chooses. Nicolas can sleep with you. I mean, I assume. Nicolas has a car, right? Can he pick up Monsieur Bloch?"

JULIEN
"Have you finished organizing the world? Now you're going to say I need to talk to Papa about this arrangement."

NATHALIE
"That would be helpful. If quarantine is coming we need to get everyone squared away. Oui? We can hardly leave Maman's 'other' husband to fend for himself."

JULIEN
"I suppose not, but I really think it would be better if you talked to Papa."

NATHALIE

"You are a coward, Julien! Never mind. I'll call Lilou and tell her to get us packed when she gets home from school and talk to Papa this afternoon. In the meantime, can you arrange for Nicolas to pick up Maman and Monsieur Bloch? And maybe Lilou, too?"

JULIEN

"Yes. Yes, I will. And a couple of cases of wine. I think we may need them."

ACT TWO

INT. - SYLVIE & HUBERT'S HOUSE - SITTING ROOM (AFTERNOON)

NATHALIE is seated on the piano bench, facing her father (HUBERT) who is slumped over in an upholstered chair with a newspaper spread across his lap. HUBERT clears his throat once, and then again, and then shakes his head at his daughter.

NATHALIE

"Come on, Papa. He's an old man. Mama can't leave him all alone in the city with this virus going around."

HUBERT

"What is this nonsense, Nathalie? No. This is my house. Monsieur Bloch should stay in his fancy apartment in the city. Not here. No."

NATHALIE

"It won't be for long, Papa. Just a week or two until they figure out testing. Then I'm sure everything will go back to normal and Monsieur Bloch will go home. He can stay in my old room. Lilou and I can sleep up in the attic."

HUBERT

"Where is Maman right now?"

NATHALIE
"She's at work, of course! This is why we need to tell her to bring Monsieur Bloch back to the house. Then she won't need to leave to check on him and we can all be safe."

HUBERT
"I keep telling her she can retire. That we don't need the money. But she insists."

NATHALIE
"I know, Papa, I know. She likes her independence. And she likes...you know...working."

HUBERT
"She likes those sob stories about Bloch's family in the concentration camps. Acts like he's some kind of hero. Like it was him suffering, and not some relative."

NATHALIE
"I think it was his mother in the camp, Papa!"

HUBERT
"Yes, well, it wasn't him, was it? Tells stories about being malnourished as a child and how he and his mother lived in poverty. Well he's quite the gourmand now! Your maman has always been such a sucker for the 'oppressed.' Oh, Jean-Pierre Bloch is SO oppressed in his deluxe flat in the Seizième. She's charmed by the sob story and impressed by the money. I am not fooled, Nathalie. I am not fooled!"

NATHALIE sighs.

HUBERT
"Do you know what she said to me, just the other week, ma fille? She said our family....my family...were probably collaborators!"

NATHALIE
"Well, Papa, who knows?"

HUBERT
"Nathalie!"

NATHALIE
"Listen, Papa, I'm sure that's very hurtful when she says things like that, but it's 2020 and there's a very bad, very contagious virus going around and we need to figure out how to keep Maman safe, at home."

HUBERT
"Why are you not having this conversation with your mother? Why not tell her she shouldn't leave the house? That she puts herself and me in jeopardy? Why not explain to her that Monsieur Bloch is fine on his own?"

NATHALIE
"Julien already tried, Papa. And you know Maman loves you very much but she also...well she is also very fond of Monsieur Bloch and it would be best for all parties to gather all of us here, together. But you are the patriarch, Papa. You. It is your decision. Whatever you say goes."

HUBERT grimaces.

HUBERT
"I don't know, Nathalie. I don't know if I can stomach...

Just then, NATHALIE's daughter (LILOU) bursts into the sitting room, followed by NICOLAS and JEAN-PIERRE. The three of them are wearing coats and carrying suitcases.

LILOU
"Salut là! Grand-père! Maman and I are staying at your house! And look, Julien's boyfriend picked me up in his Renault and we brought Papi Bloch! Mamie said she would come home on the bus so we could all fit in the car because we have two cases of wine! I guess it will be a party!"

NATHALIE
Under her breath:
"Ça c'est la meilleure!"

Out loud:
"Lilou, take our suitcase up to the attic please!"

JEAN-PIERRE takes off his hat.

JEAN-PIERRE
"Bonjour, Hubert. I cannot thank you enough for inviting me to stay in your house. Sylvie told me that you were insisting I come."

HUBERT
"Oh! She did! Well, yes...I mean, I can't be sending her off to work everyday in the middle of a pandemic so, I guess, her work must come here."

JEAN-PIERRE
"Yes...yes, of course."

Everyone looks extremely uncomfortable for an endless minute, HUBERT half out of his chair, JEAN-PIERRE still in his coat, NATHALIE with her head in her hands and NICOLAS looking for the world like he might burst out laughing. LILOU stands on the stairs to the attic clutching a carry-on suitcase and her school bag, trying to make eyes at her mother.

SYLVIE sweeps in the front door.

SYLVIE
"Alright, then! Julien stopped off at the boulangerie but I wanted to get home as soon as I could. I see everyone has arrived."

SYLVIE takes HUBERT's face in her hands and kisses him on both cheeks and then takes JEAN-PIERRE by the arm.

SYLVIE
"Come, cheri; you'll be staying in Nathalie's old room."

ACT THREE

INT. - SYLVIE & HUBERT'S HOUSE - DINING ROOM (MORNING, SEVERAL DAYS LATER)

LILOU, HUBERT, and SYLVIE are seated on one side of the dining table for breakfast. NATHALIE and JEAN-PIERRE are on the other side, with JEAN-PIERRE sitting across from SYLVIE. JEAN-PIERRE is wearing tailored pajamas that appear to be freshly ironed.
NICOLAS and JULIEN are both sitting at the head of the table. NICOLAS is sporting one of JULIEN's t-shirts, which is stretched tight across his chest. JULIEN is visibly suffering from a hangover.

JULIEN gets up to walk to the kitchen.

JULIEN
"You're looking awfully chipper this morning, Maman. No one would guess you are a frail woman in a high-risk age group, sheltering from the plague."

JEAN-PIERRE
"I'd say she looks quite radiant."

JULIEN gives both his mother and JEAN-PIERRE a sidelong glance as he carries the bowls and pitcher of hot coffee from the kitchen, followed closely by NICOLAS, wearing a tight pair of boxer briefs, who carries the pitcher of hot milk.

SYLVIE
"Despite the dangers outside, I am just so content to be here, in the house, with all of my loved ones close,"

SYLVIE smiles broadly at JEAN-PIERRE, who winks at her, and then she takes HUBERT's hand, catching him rolling his eyes across the table at NATHALIE.

NATHALIE arches an eyebrow at HUBERT.

NATHALIE
"Yes, it's so cozy, don't you agree, Papa?"

HUBERT makes a throat-clearing noise in NATHALIE's direction. He then pulls his hand from SYLVIE's and begins furiously sawing at the baguette on the cutting board next to him.

HUBERT
"Pass me the butter, will you, dear?"
Lilou is furtively texting on her mother's phone under the table and doesn't notice HUBERT speaking to her.

HUBERT
"Lilou... the butter?"

Lilou shoves the phone under her leg and then looks at her grandfather, confused.

LILOU
"Butter, Papi? I thought you weren't allowed to have butter now?"

Everyone looks in HUBERT's direction.

HUBERT
"Oh. Thank you, cheri. I don't report that you have an electronic device at the table but you feel it your place to draw attention to my request for butter? In my home? During a pandemic?"

LILOU is mortified. NATHALIE holds her hand out across the table and her daughter reluctantly hands her the phone.

NATHALIE
"You crazy child. It is not very private to text your friends on my phone!"

SYLVIE
"Julien, can you bring the muesli for Papa?"

SYLVIE pats HUBERT's shoulder, takes the bread off of his plate and puts it on her own.

SYLVIE
"And have you had your medicine this morning, Hubert?"

HUBERT looks daggers, first at SYLVIE, and then LILOU, and finally at JEAN-PIERRE, who is smiling to himself.

JEAN-PIERRE
"You are a lucky man to have such an amazing wife to care for you...so much consideration and love."
LILOU
"Where is your wife, Papi Bloch? Why aren't you married?"

NICOLAS giggles at JULIEN.

NICOLAS
"Yes, and where is your wife, mon petit?'

JULIEN sticks his tongue in NICOLAS's ear as JULIEN sets the jar of muesli on the table.

LILOU
"Dégoûtant! Make out somewhere else, you two!"'

HUBERT pours some muesli into a bowl, reaching across the table for a spoon. Then he stares at the bowl, shaking his head dolefully.

JEAN-PIERRE
"It is the great sadness in my life that I never married. I have such envy of those more fortunate than me. Those lucky enough to find their soulmates and live in wedded bliss. Every day together. Every night..."

NICOLAS snorts and JULIEN laughs uncomfortably. NATHALIE says something under her breath and LILOU pokes HUBERT, trying to make amends for ruining his breakfast. SYLVIE smiles at JEAN-PIERRE fondly but is then distracted by the large quantity of jam on his tartine.

SYLVIE
"Too much jam, Jean-Pierre. Not at all good for your blood sugar. In fact, hand that tartine to Julien; you should have some muesli, too. Hubert, mon chou, please pass Jean-Pierre the muesli."

JEAN-PIERRE's grin disappears. He clutches his tartine. HUBERT looks with disbelief at his wife. He stands up, his chair tipping back against the wall with a bang. His face turns bright red.

HUBERT
"Non. Non, non, non. It is too much to ask! I will not give him the muesli! You, monsieur, cannot have my muesli! It is mine. My muesli."

JEAN-PIERRE
"That is fine, Hubert, I certainly do not want your muesli!"

JEAN-PIERRE holds his tartine to his chest.

HUBERT
"Well good, because you will not have it!"

HUBERT sits down again, his chair legs bumping back down to the floor. For several minutes, no one says anything. Then SYLVIE pours some muesli into a bowl and pushes it across the table to JEAN-PIERRE.

Both men sadly spoon the cereal from their bowls to their mouths, and breakfast table chatter resumes.

ACT FOUR

EXT. - SYLVIE & HUBERT'S HOUSE - BACK GARDEN (AFTERNOON, ONE MONTH LATER)

The scene is planted vegetable and flower beds, and the remains of lunch on a table where NATHALIE sits, reading. Beyond her is NICOLAS, lying on the grass with his head on a rolled up sweat-

er, blowing smoke rings, with HUBERT and JEAN-PIERRE in the background on a petanque terrain. HUBERT tosses his boule and it knocks JEAN-PIERRE's boule wide of the cochonnet.

JEAN-PIERRE
"Son-of-a-bitch."

HUBERT gives a little snort, but his eyes are devoid of humor as he sits down on the bench next to JEAN-PIERRE.

NICOLAS, still lying on the grass, inhales deeply on his ciga-rette. Both older men look on wistfully at the rising smoke rings, watching them float up and expand, finally dissipating in the spring air.
HUBERT
"Sylvie made me give up smoking,"

JEAN-PIERRE
"Yes, same."

HUBERT gives JEAN-PIERRE a side-eye.

HUBERT
"I used to eat butter, smoke to my heart's content, and live with my beautiful wife, without outsiders."

JEAN-PIERRE laughs.

JEAN-PIERRE
"You still live with your beautiful wife; be grateful."

JEAN-PIERRE pulls himself to his feet and tosses the next boule. He misses HUBERT's boule but manages to get closer to the cochonnet.

HUBERT
"You live with her, too, you old coquin."

JEAN-PIERRE
"Yeah, a good lot it's doing me."

HUBERT
"Saving you from the plague, at least."

JEAN-PIERRE
"Yes, but I may die from a broken heart."

HUBERT
"So true, so true. And me, too."

JEAN-PIERRE
"Your turn."

HUBERT stays seated and turns to NICOLAS.

HUBERT
"Nicolas, how did you meet my son? And wouldn't you rather fall in love with Nathalie? She's so much prettier, and comes ready-equipped with a child."

NICOLAS rolls over on his belly and looks seriously at HUBERT.

NICOLAS
"Nathalie is very lovely, but the challenge is that she's a woman. Not really my flavor. Plus, Julien has such an excellent ass."

JEAN-PIERRE laughs.

NICOLAS
"Seriously, though, Père Hubert, I'm happy to report how Julien and I met, it's a very proper story. It was at a fundraiser for Soleil Rouge, and I was smitten by his sweet smile."
NICOLAS winks at JEAN-PIERRE.

JEAN-PIERRE
"Oh, I've heard about Soleil Rouge...the hospital clowns, right?"

NICOLAS
"Exact. I had to be there because of my position at the Health Ministry and Julien was there..."

NATHALIE
"Let me guess. Because one of his clown friends was performing?"

NICOLAS smiles and nods, blowing another smoke ring.

NATHALIE
"I wish we had some of those clowns here, now, to entertain us. Julien's clown friend, Arnaud, is very attractive as I recall."

HUBERT
"A clown? Nathalie, you can't be serious!"

HUBERT looks at JEAN-PIERRE beside him for support.

HUBERT
"Can you understand?"

JEAN-PIERRE
"As puzzled as you...Nathalie, we think...that is, your father and I, we think that 1) you should give up this romantic interest in clowns and, 2) Nicolas should be enamored of you rather than your brother."

NATHALIE
"Hmmm, Nicolas is a little too armoire à glace for my tastes, but I hear from Julien that he has a good salary, so, you know, if you think of switching teams, Nic, I could probably hold my nose."

NICOLAS
"Absolutely, Nathalie. You'll be the first lady on my list if I give up men."

JULIEN walks into the garden from the kitchen door carrying two wine bottles in one hand and several glasses in the other.

JULIEN
"What's this I hear about you giving up men, Nicolas? Oh la la! Where does that leave me?"

JULIEN sits down on the grass next to NICOLAS and kisses him on the cheek.

NATHALIE
"Bah. These lovebirds are enough to make you sick, no?"

Both HUBERT and JEAN-PIERRE look pained.

NATHALIE
"What's wrong with you two? Sour from your Petanque war?"

LILOU sticks her head out of the kitchen door.

LILOU
"Mamie! Mamie! Mamie?"

LILOU walks out into the garden.

LILOU
"Where is Grandmère? I've been looking all over the house!"

JEAN-PIERRE
"She's out."

HUBERT
"Yes, out."

NATHALIE
"Out where? Restrictions are not lifted...where could she be?"

NICOLAS
"Apparently the grocer mentioned he'd lost his assistant..."

JULIEN
"Yes, that's right. Maman and I were there last week picking up supplies and he was going on and on about how difficult it was all on his own, and how he was unable to hire with the pandemic going on."

JEAN-PIERRE
"Probably very handsome. Younger I presume?"

HUBERT
"Guessing he likes to talk politics. Probably more Jewish than you, Bloch."

NATHALIE
"What?!? Non, non, non, not the grocer. Not during a pandemic! Not with Papa and Jean-Pierre both already here! What can she be thinking?"

JULIEN
"Maman said that everyone is quite well taken care of here, and that she could be of use to an essential, frontline service."

LILOU
"Does that mean that Mamie has gone back to work?"

HUBERT
"Or something."

NICOLAS lights another cigarette. Birdsong can be heard from the trees above their heads. No one speaks. Finally, JEAN-PIERRE starts to get up.

JEAN-PIERRE
"Well. Shall we get back to it? Is it my turn?"

HUBERT
"No, It turns out that it isn't. Not mine. And, also, not yours."

END SCENE

DALMATIA FLEMING

Dalmatia Fleming is dabbling in writing with the encouragement of kind people. It's challenging; just try, you'll improve.

THE ELLEN CHRONICLES

CHAPTER ONE

Ellen kissed Grandpa on the cheek. "Hi Grandpa."

"Hi sweetheart, how was your first day at work?"

"I'm exhausted" Ellen said as she flopped into the large, comfy chair.

"But it was good. Everyone seemed really nice, and the customers were very patient with me. I got a little confused at first, you know, keeping the waitresses' sections straight and all that."

"Well, sounds good!" said Grandpa. "And what about your schedule, did they give you one?"

"Yeah, twenty hours to start with, then they will increase me to thirty. They're easing me into it. And I think I can make some new friends too."

"Glad to hear it Ellen."

Ellen, now sitting forward in the chair, "I'm so thankful that Mac gave me a chance with this job."

"Well, he owes me one big time, so I would say we're even now. I told him you'd be perfect for this; you're very likable, at ease around strangers, and the young guys from far and wide will be stopping by to check out the new girl in town! And they won't be disappointed! Business will be booming!"

"HA! Thanks Grandpa! But I think you're partial. Maybe I should call Mac, or write him a letter to say thank you?"

"That would be nice."

"I mean, after all, I'm not really sixteen, fifteen and a half to be exact."

"Close enough."

"Yeah... I'm starved!"

"Don't you get a free meal on work days?"

"Yeah, but I totally forgot!"

So began Ellen's new job as a hostess at Claire's, the neighborhood diner. She started to make friends there, that is, in the little free time she had to visit with her co-workers and customers. This was the hub of the neighborhood.

As time passed, personal questions would be asked of Ellen. Not that they were invasively personal questions, just the kind that people ask as they're getting to know someone. People just liked her and wanted to know a little bit more about her, the same sort of questions that she would ask of others. Still, she wasn't sure how long she could stall without looking like she had something to hide.

"Hey, Grandma?"

"Yeah Hon."

"People are asking me where my parents are, do I have any brothers and sisters, why am I staying with Grandma and Grandpa, where am I from… what am I going to say?"

"Well… let me think about tha… whatever you do, DON'T tell them the truth."

"OK… but what should I say?"

"Well… maybe you can say that your family was part of a missionary abroad, and that your parents and siblings are still 'there', and that you wanted to experience American life so you came here to live with Grandma and Grandpa. That's true, isn't it?"

"Yeah, I guess I COULD explain it like that. But I don't want to stand out. I don't want to be different."

"Well, Ellen, look how well you're adapting to your job and everything else. You're a true success story. We both know that is often not the case. The fact that you're doing so well just goes to show how much you've got going for yourself."

"Thanks Grandma… but… really, I just want to be like everyone else and have nothing to hide."

"You don't have anything to hide, you just have to frame what you say in a way that other people can understand."

"But I resent having to do that. No one else has to do that. It's not fair!"

"Hon, everyone puts a little spin on everything they say. Everyone wants to look good to other people and tells 'little white lies' every now and then if it makes their life easier."

"Yeah, but I'm just afraid I'm going to let my guard down and screw up."

"You won't. Anyway, the more time passes and the more people get to know you, the less surprised they'll be if you accidentally 'spill the beans' so to speak."

Ellen sighed. "Yeah, I guess you're right."

Two Months Later at Claire's

Tiffany sidled up to Gracie at the warming station by the kitchen, "Gracie?"

"Yeah?"

"What time do you get off tonight?"

"Nine."

"Me too. Wait for me and let's walk out together."

"OK."

Nine o'clock came and went. The girls met and left together.

"Gracie, you're not gonna believe this. Ellen and I went to a movie last night and I found out about her mysterious past."

"Yeah?"

"Yeah. She used to live in some weird religious cult. It was a commune."

"Wow. That's what Jimmy and Sara were thinking."

"Yeah. She escaped and came to live with her grandparents who she barely knew. Never met them in her life until she came here. She only wrote letters and got birthday and Christmas presents from them."

"I'm glad she got out, how creepy!"

"I know. I guess she was disgusted with the whole thing, and scared too. There was a lot of sexual abuse going on, with the girls.

"Gross. Did she say if any bad things happened to her?"

"She didn't say. But I'm guessing that they did. Pretty sure they did."

"Why do you say that?"

"Because she's trying to convince her two sisters to leave. She's gotta huge family back there, something like two sisters and five brothers."

"Ugh, good. So does this mean she's disowned by her family or something? I'm guessing her parents aren't happy about this."

"Not sure. We didn't talk about that and she didn't let on about it."

"Wow... you know, I would have never guessed she came from this weird background except for the unanswered questions. I mean, she seems so normal otherwise."

"I know. How could she be so normal?"

One Week Later at Grandma and Grandpa's House

"Hi sweetie… what's with the long face? How was work today?"

"Oh Grandpa, I think everyone at work knows!"

"Knows what?"

"You know!"

"Oh… why do you say that?"

"They're acting all weird, that's why!"

"Well, did you tell them anything?"

"Just one girl, Tiffany. I just know she told everyone! I can feel it! Ever since then it's been different."

"Well, sweetie, you've made lots of friends there. People like you. They like you for who you are."

"I don't know about that. They think I'm different, not like them. I don't want to be different."

"I'm not so sure … you've made a fresh start here. You've moved on. Does it really matter? Come here, let Grandpa give you a hug."

Ellen rushed over to the comfort of Grandpa's hug. "Yeah… I guess."

Another Week Later

"BESSIE… BESSS-SIEEE… "

Bessie dropped her book and rushed into the kitchen to find Earl, Ellen's Grandfather, holding a piece of paper. "What … what?"

"I think Ellen's left… look." Earl held up a note. "She left this and looks like most of her things are gone." Bessie took the note from Earl and read it out loud:

"Dear Grandma and Grandpa,

"I can't stay here anymore. I have to go back. I'm too homesick and my job is not working out anymore. I'm positive everyone knows. I'm really uncomfortable now.

"I love you both so much and am so thankful for all you have done for me. I'll come back, but I can't stay here any longer right now. Maybe in a few years I can break away for real.

"All my love,

"Ellen"

CHAPTER TWO

Ellen made the long trip from Grandma and Grandpa's house back to her family. It was good to see them again, she had missed them. But she couldn't stand being back in the cult and felt like a failure for not being strong enough to leave for good.

Her parents seemed happy to see her but they were guarded. Everyone in the cult was acting that way towards her. No mention was made of her having left and returned whatsoever. Not even to rub it in. Ellen expected that. It was as though she never left. Only her siblings and a few others secretly ask her what it was like out there: what was it like at Grandma and Grandpa's house, did she get a job, did she make friends easily, what were the people like; questions like these.

Leaving the cult seemed impossible while in it. Everyone knew that few had the connections or skills required to survive "out there". After all, only English was spoken in the cult, they were never taught the language of the country where they lived. They picked up a little here and there, but integration into the local culture was not part of the cult's plan. In fact, it was quite the opposite. This left those born into the cult extremely dependent on it; it was the only thing they knew. The only time cult members interacted with the locals was to ask them for handouts.

Ellen immediately began to plan her next escape.

About a year and a half later Ellen left again, but this time she didn't venture quite so far geographically. She simply left the cult and moved to the big city. Here she again landed a job as a hostess, but this time at an elite club frequented by successful businessmen. Her tall height, slender build and strawberry blond hair made her a standout in this locale and surely played a part in securing this position.

Ellen quickly picked up the language. Soon she had a good rapport with the regulars and was working all they busy nights. She also became quite a draw; the regulars would bring their friends to see the beautiful and exotic young foreigner.

Business was good and Ellen earned a lot in tips. She shared a tiny two- bedroom apartment with a young local woman, Yasuko, who worked first shift as a nurse. Yasuko was trying to make it on her own as well and had her own challenges to overcome. They could relate to each other and became fast friends. Most days there were a few hours between their respective work shifts and they would hang out in the apartment together, talk about their dreams and obstacles and always have a few good laughs.

"Yasuko, I don't know if I said or did something, but I get the feeling this guy wants me to perform sexual favors for him. Maybe for his friends too. It's creeping me out."

"What's he doing; why do you say that?"

"Well, he started to run his hand up and down my back and sort of pats me. I have to be nice to him, he's a customer. And he has started to give me bigger tips as well. I think he wants something."

"It sounds that way, doesn't it?"

"Yeah. Then, he keeps bringing in new friends, different men all the time. He makes a point of introducing me to them. I don't like the way they're looking at me."

"Sorry about that Ellen. Can you think of anything, ANYTHING that you did differently or said before this started that may have given him the wrong idea?"

"Well... I remember that I complemented him on his new suit one day. He always wore a black suit, white shirt and dark colored tie. Then one day he came in wearing this mossy green suit with a black turtleneck. He looked so much more hip than usual. And I told him so... oh... so he thinks I'm interested in him?"

"That's probably it. Single women NEVER tell men they look attractive. It's just not done here."

"Well, I didn't tell him he looked attractive ... I think."

"It doesn't matter, you've said too much. He thinks you're waving him in."

"Well I was just trying to be friendly and make small talk. That's part of my job."

One Week Later

"Yasuko, Mr. Inagawa tried to corner me in front of the elevator. I think he was trying to get me in there. I managed to squirm away by saying I had to attend to the group who just walked through the door. I'm starting to run out of excuses to get away from this guy. I think I'm going to have to tell my manager."

"No, don't do that!"

"Why not? I don't have to put up with this crap. Besides, this whole thing is really creeping me out."

"But you can't do that. You have no rights here to do that. You'll lose your job."

"Lose my job, are you kidding!?"

Another Week Later

"Yasuko, Inagawa invited me to a film set, or that's what it sounds like anyway. I know he has a friend who's involved with movies."

"Don't go!"

"Well, of course I'm not going!"

"What's this movie-guy's name anyway?"

"Um... Namaguchi?"

"Yamaguchi?"

"Yes, that's it."

"That's the Yakuza! DON'T GO!"

"I'm not, I'm not! This... this is getting crazy!"

Two days later

"Yasuko, I'm leaving and going back to the US. I checked my bank account and I've saved a ton of money. I've gotta get out of here. Got my ticket, I'm leaving tomorrow."

"What, so soon?"

"Yeah. In the meantime, I'm calling in sick. The creepy thing is that Mr. Inagawa knows where I live, so that means Yamaguchi probably does as well. I'm getting so paranoid; I wouldn't be surprised if they showed up here. So please keep all the blinds closed and don't open the door for anyone until I'm outta here."

"Of course, Ellen."

"Why don't you come with me?"

"Well...?"

CHAPTER THREE

Ellen settled into southern California. The large sum of money she saved while working as a hostess at an elite club in Tokyo enabled her to cover her rent and tuition at a community college without having to work. Ellen did more than just survive, she thrived. She passed the GED exam and a couple of years later, graduated with an Associate's degree. After a few entry level jobs, Ellen landed a position at a prominent tech company. The hours were long, but Ellen was determined to assimilate into American society no matter what.

Ellen's little brother Chuck was the next of her siblings to leave the cult. He kept in close contact with Ellen ever since her move to California. Ellen did all she could to encourage Chuck to leave.

Eventually Chuck was able to make it to the American east coast and stay with his grandparents, as Ellen had done, until the time came for him to join the military. Chuck was angry, and the military provided sanctioned violence which he needed at that time; boot camp, guns, fighting and an enemy. Chuck got kicked out after about a year and a half after he got in a brawl in a bar parking lot over a girl. The police found a gun in his car and Chuck went to jail for three months. When he got out, he moved to California to live with Ellen.

Ellen put in a good word for Chuck with one of her previous employers and Chuck was able to land an entry level job.

Ellen and Chuck settled in to American life and their time in the cult seemed almost like a past life, very distant indeed. Until one day when Ellen received a phone call from their dad.

"Hey, Chuck?"

"Yeah?"

"Dad called yesterday. He's coming to town and wants to see us."

"Oh, so the Asshole wants to see us, huh? Like, raising us in a 'hippy Jesus commune' and almost ruining our lives wasn't enough for him, he has to come back and see us? I could go the rest of my life without seeing that pervert again."

"I know, but we could at least meet him. You know I'm not looking forward to it either."

"Yeah, I know."

"What do you think, should we meet him in a public place, like a restaurant, or should I invite him over here?"

"We better meet him in public. If he comes over here I might beat the shit out of him. I'm older and bigger now, and in a lot better shape since I last saw him. He's probably a shriveled up old man now."

"He's not an 'old' man."

"Yeah, well, I could beat him to a pulp."

"OK, so it's decided then, we'll meet him in public."

Ellen sent her dad a text message and suggested they meet at a neighborhood Japanese restaurant. He agreed and they set the date, two days from now.

Ellen and Chuck arrived at the restaurant forty-five minutes early. They needed to get a head start on the sake. Chuck motioned to the waitress. "Miss, may we have another tokkuri of sake please?"

"Chuck, no... That's OK Miss; we'll wait until the rest of our party arrives."

Chuck glared at Ellen. "You don't have to drink it now if you don't want to." Chuck was fidgeting in his seat, his foot tapping the floor nervously.

"Chuck, you need to calm down ... look at you, you're a nervous wreck, and angry. I don't want you drunk when dad gets here. I want to be able to steer the conversation, I can't control it when you're like that."

"YOU can't control it when I'M like THAT? Since when do you think it's YOUR job to control things, especially ME! You should be THANKING me. Remember, I'm the one who told mom. He let those hippy Jesus perverts rape you. RAPE YOU Ellen, that's what is was you know!"

Ellen leaned forward and said in a hushed voice "I know what it was and you need to keep your voice down."

"Everything OK over here?" ask the waitress.

"Yes, we're fine, thank you" said Ellen.

"Yes, we're fine, thank you" Chuck mocked under his breath while glaring at Ellen. "Yeah, where fine all right. Just move to another continent, bury our heads in our work, suppress everything and pretend it never happened. Sometimes I think I'm gonna explode. I could kill that bastard."

"I know, I know." Ellen paused, she could feel her heart racing. Perspiration began to appear on her forehead. She looked down and realized she had shredded her paper napkin all over her lap. She blushed and nervously brushed it off.

There was a long silence. Ellen glanced up to find Chuck staring at her. She quickly looked away. "You're right. I have SO blocked this out of my memory. Look at me, I'm shaking." Ellen held her hands above the table and stared at them, and then self-consciously put them back on her lap. "This is going to be hard. Hey Chuck, will you pour me some sake please?"

Chuck looked hard at Ellen's face, then filled her ochoko, a large thimble-sized cup. Ellen stared at it in silence. She took a sip, eyes still turned downward. Chuck slowly extended his hand across the table. Ellen stared at it, then reached out to hold it. Ellen looked up and their gaze locked.

The light surrounding them dimmed as a shadow began to slowly envelop their space. They looked up.

"Hey kids... oh my God... great to see you!"

"Hey Dad." Ellen stood up walked the few steps towards dad, standing there with outstretched arms, and hugged him. Dad hugged her tightly, a big bear hug. Ellen almost felt like he would crush her.

"Honey, how long has it been?" Dad held her back at arm's length. "Look at you! All grown up and so beautiful!"

"Yeah, well" Ellen said embarrassedly. There was a seemingly long silence.

"Sit down Dad" Ellen said while motioning towards the table where Chuck was still sitting, his expression not very welcoming.

"Chuck!" Dad, again with the outstretched arms moved towards Chuck as if to hug him as well, but Chuck interrupted by quickly and stiffly offering his hand instead.

"Oh, well, great to see you Chuck." They shook hands, dad overly enthusiastically. "Wow, you are a very fit young man. Ha, ha, I sure wouldn't want to bump into you in a dark alley, ha, ha!"

"Hi Dad." Chuck pulled his hand back and sat down.

Ellen jumped right in, "Dad, please have a seat." Dad sat down followed by Ellen. "Here, let's make a toast," Ellen said. She poured both Dad's and Chuck's sake, as is customary in Japan, then she poured her own. Ochoko raised, they toasted in unison "Kanpai." Then Dad added "To my beautiful children, empowered by their personal relationship with God to enlighten the world, and to share the good news of God's love."

Ellen and Chuck's eyes met, their gaze locked.

Dad didn't waste a second. "It's so great that you two were able to fit yourselves into my busy schedule. I kind of worried for a moment that this meet up wouldn't happen, but being the great kids that you are ... ha, ha, here we are!"

Ellen, smiling while looking at Chuck... "Yes Dad WE'RE glad it worked out, aren't we Chuck."

Chuck said nothing.

Dad, oblivious continued "Well, the Fellowship has been keeping me very busy lately... yes... very busy indeed. Between all the inspirational stuff, you know, the educational publications and movies... you know, the cartoon series, that's what I'm talking about; we've produced some very popular ones. Those have won awards you know. What else... oh yeah, then there's the pod-casts. We have a lot of those. Don't know off the top of my head if those have won any awards. I'm partial to the cartoon series, ha, ha. And now, with the help of one of our key sponsors, we're compiling all of those original songs, there must be thousands of them, well maybe hundreds. No, I think thousands. Remember those songs?"

"Uh... yes Dad" said Ellen.

Chuck squirmed and turned away, looking at nothing in particular.

"We had some very talented people in the Fellowship didn't we? You know they composed those songs, they made them up, you know?"

"Yes Dad, I know what composed means" said Ellen.

"Oh yeah, ha, ha. Well, I can barely keep up with all this, I'm so busy. So now we're compiling them to be released... for sale! We're re-mixing them... is that what you call it? You know, upgrading the sound quality?"

"Yes, remixing" said Ellen.

"Ha, ha, obviously not my specialty. So they will be better than ever. We even have a few with children's voices singing the chorus. Hey, you kids are probably singing on some of those. What do you think about that? You can tell you friends you made a recording!"

"Well, hey, look at us," Ellen said jokingly.

"So, what do you think Ellen, could pull a few strings and get these things in iTunes?"

Chuck jumped out of his chair, "What the Hell ... is that what this meet up is all about? You could care less about seeing us. You're just trying to manipulate Ellen to help sell your cult shit!"

"Chuck... calm down" Ellen said slowly and quietly as she started to raise from her chair to reach for Chuck's arm.

"I AM calm," Chuck yelled as he jerked his arm away from Ellen. "That's it, we're getting the Hell outta here. As long as I'm around your days of manipulating Ellen are OVER!" Now Chuck grabbed Ellen's arm. "Come on Ellen!"

CHAPTER FOUR

"And here is your key. I think you will like this room. It has a wonderful view of the city."

"Thank you; I do enjoy a good view. Good evening."

"Good evening Miss Koenig. Best wishes for a successful business meeting."

"Thank you."

Ellen turned and looked out upon the massive hotel lobby, beautifully appointed with just the right mix of traditional and modern Japanese design. Noticing she had dropped her wallet, Ellen bent down to pick it up and upon arising, felt light headed. She paused for a moment to let it pass, assuming it was due to jet lag. She made her way to the elevator and up to the 53rd floor. Her room was at the end of the long corridor.

Ellen opened the door to room #5379 and as she walked in, was immediately confronted with a most spectacular view of Tokyo. Ellen quickly deposited her luggage and slowly walked over to the window as if in a trance. Feeling light headed again, she reached out for the back of a large chair to steady herself and then to sit down. She melted into the high backed, upholstered chair, her body becoming completely limp.

Ellen gazed out among the towering buildings and dazzling lights against the black backdrop of the night sky. The view before her seemed to move in and out of focus; lights at one moment the size of precise little pinheads and the next large and blurry as though looking through a window in the pouring rain. She could hear the city hum, even thought she heard individual voices. She thought she heard her name. Ellen struggled to regain control of herself.

It was 10:30 p.m. Ellen needed to get to bed. She was partnership director—Asia for a leading software corporation and was about to lead a very important business workshop. The first meeting started at 7 a.m. and she had already lost a night's sleep due to the long flight and time change. Ellen rose from the chair, still unsteady on her feet. She managed to brush her teeth, pull off a few articles of clothing, drop them on the floor, and fall into bed.

It was not a restful night for Ellen. She tossed and turned all night. At one point, she awoke drenched in sweat, her skin cold and clammy. She pulled off her remaining wet clothing and rolled over to the other side of the king-sized bed where it seemed warmer. She managed to fall back to sleep only to experience one odd dream after another, each one progressively unsettling compared to the last.

Promptly at 6 a.m., the phone rang. It was her wake-up call. Ellen arose and readied herself for the day's meeting as if on autopilot.

Now she could see the city scape in the twilight. She paused for one last look. The buildings and landmarks were beginning to look familiar; she was beginning to get her bearings. She felt less out of control now. But what did it all mean... the odd sensations of the previous evening... the dreams, so disturbing at the time which she could now barely remember. Ellen struggled to make sense of it. She left her room and headed down to the hotel conference room.

During the lunch break, her Japanese counterpart, Mr. Nakamura, approached her to chat.

"Miss Koenig, you have done a wonderful job. I am very excited about the potential partnership of our two companies. I can't wait to get started again after lunch."

"By the way, my company has a nice evening planned for you and your team tonight. I hope you all will be able to attend. We would like to make everything as easy and comfortable as possible and have arranged for a fleet of Limos to transport you and your team to one of our finest restaurants. My team will be attending as well."

"Well, thank you so much Mr. Nakamura. I'm looking forward to it. I'm sure my team will be thrilled as well."

The day's meetings ended and the two teams gathered in the hotel lobby. This first day had gone well. Everyone was more than ready for a pleasant evening out. Up pulled the fleet of limos; everyone hopped in and off they went.

It was now dark outside. As the others talked, Ellen turned away and began to focus more on the streetscape outside the limo. She now knew exactly where they were. She was afraid she knew exactly where they were headed.

Fifteen minutes later, the fleet of limos pulled over and stopped. Ellen swallowed hard and discretely dabbed at the beads of perspiration that had formed on her forehead.

Ellen's fears were confirmed. Here they were, at the restaurant that housed the elite club where she had once worked as a hostess; were the men disturbingly eyed her and more; where she had no right to expect for it to be any other way.

"What should I do"?! Ellen thought. Ten years had passed. Perhaps everything was different now; the management had changed, the clientele had changed, everything had changed... please!

Ellen was trying to act as though everything was fine. Her group looked up to her. She had to set the tone for the evening. Ellen was never quite comfortable in this leadership role. She was promoted due to her technical abilities as is often the case, and felt somewhat like an imposter when it came to being "in charge".

Ellen's team was gathering their belongings, joking around in the cramped quarters of the limo, preparing to enjoy the evening.

Ellen opened her handbag, remembering her hair bun making tool, and instantly twirled her strawberry blond hair into an elegant and stylish bun. At least she might be unrecognizable with her hair this way, just in case nothing had changed. The dress code during Ellen's tenure was to wear one's long hair down at all times.

They walked up to the front door. It looked exactly the same. The name of the restaurant had not changed.

Upon entering, Ellen paused to look in the direction of the elite club room and saw an attractive tall young hostess with a distinctive Scandinavian look. This was not a good sign, Ellen thought; still an "attractive foreigner" as hostess. Meanwhile, the rest of the group was led back to a large private party room. Ellen hurried to catch up.

Ellen's team was all big eyes; the décor of the room was exquisite. There were twelve large round tables; each seat was labeled with a place card to ensure the two groups would mix and socialize. Everyone eventually found their seat and sat down. Ellen was sitting next to Mr. Nakamura, her counterpart.

"Miss Koenig, it seems that your team members are enjoying themselves, I'm so glad."

"Yes, this is a beautiful place. They all worked so hard preparing for these meetings. They could use a little down time. Thank you for inviting us."

"It's my pleasure. You know, the owner is here tonight. I will try to find him. I'm sure he would be very pleased to meet you and your team."

"We would be pleased to meet him as well" Ellen said, but thinking that she knew who it would be and hoping that if she was correct, that he would not recognize her. "Please excuse me for a moment Mr. Nakamura."

"Oh... now don't wander too far."

"I won't."

Ellen left the room and quickly walked back to the lobby. Looking around, she saw a display of travel brochures; so she took one, pretending to read it. Nose-in-brochure she lingered, discretely observing the hostess to the elite club and her interactions with the male clients.

Just then, two groups of men entered in quick succession. She studied the hostess's face and body language and could immediately sense her pain.

Then a third group entered, the largest group. This group looked familiar to Ellen. Yes... there they were... it was Mr. Inagawa and Mr. Yamaguchi, the Yakuza Godfather! Ellen's skin crawled as she observed the same behaviors she wished she could forget. They all disappeared and the hostess returned a few minutes later.

Ellen approached her. "Hi I'm Ellen. I'm visiting from America on business." Ellen reached out and shook her hand.

"Nice to meet you, I'm Ingrid."

Ellen looked around, "This is a beautiful place Ingrid, have you worked here long?"

"About a year and a half. I'm saving money for school; the tips are very good here."

"Great, well, you keep saving then. And where would you like to go to school?"

"I have cousins in America, in a few cities; that's where I want to go. But I really don't where I should go to school."

Ellen leaned in and began to speak in a hushed voice. "You know Ingrid, I once worked here. At your very job. I was also saving money to go to school in America."

Ingrid pulled back and studied Ellen's face. "Hey, you're the one!"

"The one?"

"Yeah, you're the one who got out! I've heard all about you. Everyone talks about you, discretely of course."

"Oh, OK... Well... I'm glad you've been able to save money. I bet you're about ready to start school then? I work in the tech industry. Is that of any interest to you?"

"Um, it could be."

"Here's my card. And here's the hotel where I'm staying. We have four more days of our business conference. Why don't you stop. We can have lunch; you can observe part of the conference and see what you think."

"I will. Oh, thank you Ellen, thank you."

"It's my pleasure Ingrid. I better get back before anyone suspects something."

"Of course."

Ellen hurried down the hallway; soft voices and laughter growing louder as she approached their private party room. Ellen entered and gracefully slid into her chair; it seemed as though no one had even noticed she was gone. A few moments later, Mr. Nakamura turned in her direction.

"There you are! I was afraid we lost you!"

"Well, I stopped by the ladies' room, then got a little lost."

"I'm glad you found us! And just in time to meet the owner, Mr. Shimojima. Mr. Shimojima, I would like for you to meet Miss Koenig."

"Pleased to meet you,, Miss Koenig" he said, shaking her hand.

"Pleased to meet you too, Mr. Shimojima," Ellen said, acting as though she had never met him before.

Mr. Shimojima appeared to be deep in thought, studying Ellen's face.

CHAPTER FIVE

Ellen took a sip of coffee. It was lukewarm. Instantaneously she was transported back to reality; this coffee tasted awful. She realized that her stomach was not feeling quite right, kind of acidic, probably from drinking this terrible coffee without having breakfast. Ellen figured she better eat something. Anticipating this day had made her anxious, dampening her appetite so she didn't eat. Ellen opened her large shoulder bag and found some crackers. She ate some.

Ellen picked up her phone to text her husband. "Hi Mark. On second train now. I'm nervous! I'll meet you at the restaurant around 7:30 for dinner. Have a fun day! Xo E".

Ellen looked out the window of the train. The landscape looked familiar, yet different. It had been twenty years since she was last here and the circumstances were very different then. She heard that the compound in which she had grown up was now a botanical garden. This relieved her a little; maybe it wouldn't be so hard to face her past life after all. Perhaps all the bad cult mojo had been broken down to atomic particles, rearranged into nutrients and consumed by beautiful plants... maybe?

Ellen nervously assembled her things in preparation to leave the train. She checked her phone for messages. Mark had answered back; "Hey E. You'll be awesome. Remember what your counselor said. Now you can move forward. Xoxo M."

The five-minute warning whistle blew, and people began to work their way towards the door. Ellen noticed three adults fussing over about thirty kids, all about the same age. Ellen figured it must be a class field trip. The kids were cute, so innocent looking. Ellen thought back to when she was their age. Suddenly she was beginning to wonder if this was such a good idea after all.

The door to the train opened and everyone began to file out. Ellen held back a little and watched them all exit, watched the teachers gathering up the kids.

"Miss, is this your stop?" the steward asked.

"Um... yes, it is. Thank you."

Ellen exited the train. She turned and looked back. The steward gave her a big smile and waved. How nice to not be fearful, Ellen thought. She smiled and waved back. The train pulled away.

There was the entrance. It looked peaceful enough. Was it a trap? Ellen dabbed at the perspiration that had formed on her forehead and slowly walked forward. "One ticket please.... Thank you." Ellen walked through the gate.

It was beautiful, so far anyway. The plantings were very lush, with blown glass sculptural forms artfully intermingled with the plants. Wow, Ellen thought. What a change. It was so sparse in the cult days.

Ellen picked up a trifold pamphlet and opened it. Inside was a map of the garden. Ellen studied it. It looked to be the same layout that Ellen remembered. It had been a school campus before being donated to the cult, so Ellen had been told. The map reflected that sort of arrangement and feeling. Ellen looked around. But the buildings looked different; they no longer looked like the bunkers of Ellen's memory. There was a lot more glass.

The garden café and gift shop had been the cult mess hall. Ellen's mom had spent hours there preparing breakfast, lunch, and dinner for hundreds of cult members. Ellen's former dormitory, the children were separated from their parents in the cult, was now a desert vivarium. Ellen decided to go there first.

The old dormitory was almost completely glass now; as much concrete was removed as was possible while keeping it structurally sound. Ellen could see cacti—some that looked familiar, and some exotic-looking ones she had never seen before. It reminded her of the area surrounding her current home in Southern California. "Well, maybe I should go inside," Ellen thought.

Upon entering, Ellen could feel the sudden change to arid air with her first breath. And the heat. It felt good on her skin. Ellen slowly began to walk through the displays. She saw some reptiles, some that reminded her of the ones at home and again, some exotic looking ones.

Was this the theme for the day? Maybe the theme for more than just this day? Everything was the same and different at the same time. She was the same person, but different after twenty years had passed. This place was the same but different compared to before. And truly better than before. The cult was gone, nowhere to be seen; and Ellen decided right then that the cult would no longer have a grip on her. She would be free of it.

Ellen saw the teachers and school children. She approached them and started up a conversation in their native language, although Ellen was a little rusty. The children giggled at her attempt to speak their language. Ellen laughed as well.

Ellen pulled out her phone to text Mark: "Hey Mark. A-OK over here. Maybe I can meet you sooner. I think I'll leave earlier than planned. Check your phone. Xo E."

TOM GAFFNEY

Tom Gaffney began on a fish-shaped island and later found himself in Seattle, where he continues. He likes the smell of peat and to occasionally sleep on a glacier. Unfortunately, he has not yet visited Saturn or any of its moons.

CORNELIUS WANDERS — I

Headphones donned and phone located, he dives into the music and the rain at the same time. "Living easy, living free. Season ticket on a one way ride." His niece, Cissy, had shared the playlist with him today. Apparently she has discovered AC-DC. She too is now on the Highway to Hell. Well, if Cissy's going, perhaps I'll go, or return.

He had savored the last bit of his whiskey and then the last third of his pint. "Goodnight", he wished to Brendan, and with mutual nods off he went.

Standing at Kate-Pat's outer door, he got cozy in his big super-duper rainy day coat. Oils, that's what they called them here when he was a kid. Perfect for the days when it was so wet nothing else would keep you dry. He notes some exposed pants below the bottom of the coat and the top of his shoes. He observes the rain moving sideways and accepts the possibility of wet legs and feet long before he gets back to Paddy's place. His place now.

Immediately immersed in the riff and the memory and what? How many detailed critiques of AC-DC songs have been written? Any? He begins attempting to assess the overall impact this simple ditty has had on his life; how many times has he listened to it? The night he first heard it, that notable evening, a definite point of demarcation, a clear before and after.

Wary of sentimentality and nostalgia and thought processes and anything that would take him back to Long Island, he walked the rainy lane in the back of beyond—Milltown, nestled in a triangle between Belturbet, Butler's Bridge, and Ballyconnell. Surely you've heard of it?

Is it acceptable to skip the rest of the song? To change the playlist? Knowing the answer is no—at least in terms of personal protocol—Corny returns to the basic argument of who cares? If you don't like it, just change the song.

"Asking nothing, leave me be. Taking everything in my stride."

But of course, that's too simple. It implies an arrogance about the course of events, the course you think they will take. In other words, changing the song ignores superstition about changing the song. Silly analyses abound, and you haven't even gotten back to the stash. In the hay shed. Go narrowback, go.

Rules are rules: one, if Cissy asks, you do it. Two, the veto of a song has to come before it starts. This is his rule, he takes it for granted at this moment. His thought digressions on this subject do not interest him now (but they are lengthy). Three, though Cissy does not know it (her parents might), the song was part of a departure. Once. And thirty years ago he had listened to it so much it was trite.

Anyway. It was December 1983. Corny was the same age then as Cissy is now. Mom and Dad were traveling. Can you believe they farmed me out at that tender age? But gone they were, a little pre-Christmas long weekend added to the father unit's business trip. Too much of a chance to pass up. I get it—they were tired of all that parenting stuff, for the most part. They had done a lot of it.

But what to do with me, the runt of the batch?

Desperate times had called for questionable measures they might later lament, but off I went to Richard's house. Dad's second cousin once removed, or something like that. Richard was younger than Dad, lived with his two brothers in Babylon. They would keep an eye on me for the weekend. I loved Richard, mainly because he had an Atari and I got as much time as I wanted on it when I was at his house. Pete and Owen were alright too, but Richard was the leader. Fun, coarse, drove a beat up truck, chain smoked. His house was always a mess. A house for overgrown boys, and he was the oldest.

He picked me up after school and whisked me to his place. Set me down in front of the TV with some pizza. Asteroids, Defender, Space Invaders, pizza and Coke Classic: the perfect Friday night. I woke up in the bean bag sometime around 2:00 a.m. if the clock was to be believed.

The three of them were at the kitchen table, passing around a bong and laughing.

"The family is moving," Richard said. "The house is empty—or almost empty. I'm just being curious, taking a look around, you never know what you are going to find. And there they were sitting with old napkins and Chinese food menus."

Four tickets to AC-DC on Sunday night at the Coliseum.

"It's like Pennies from Heaven," said Pete.

"More like fucking awesome," said Owen. "I hadn't even thought about going, too much money, too much hassle."

"But there they were, in an envelope with 'Happy Birthday Ede' written on the outside."

"But the family is gone."

"Gone," echoed Owen. "Not a thing you can do."

"Except go to the show!"

Richard is an interior painter. Keeps himself and his brothers and a group of other guys working and generally out of trouble. Someone had bought a new house and he was painting the inside before they moved in. Not even a moral question: the people are gone, the tickets there for the taking. If not him, someone else will grab them.

"Who are we giving the fourth ticket to?"

"We are going to take Corny. He's a part of the tribe this weekend."

"Can you take a kid to an AC-DC show?"

"No age on the tickets."

"I don't know," said Pete. "Could be frightening—for him or us."

"Look, he is ours for the weekend. He can be a part of everything. He will be."

AC-DC, I thought to myself. Hmmm. A concert. Perhaps this event, a big event from my peer group's standpoint, could enhance my social standing? I doubt it, but it couldn't hurt. Another thing about Richard and his brothers were that they were the only males I knew where the fact that I set all the high scores on their videos games was good enough for them. Impressive. They thought I was as cool as I did. That's one place anyway.

I must have fallen back to sleep. I woke up late the next day, continued gaming. Eventually Richard got up, took me out for KFC. Broke the news to me. Was I up for it? Could I handle the big show?

I assured him I was. We still had a day and a bit before the show. He even told me I could skip school on Monday: we would be out late. The intervening time—from Saturday afternoon—was passed in a haze of video games, junk food, soda, weed smoke. The house was an amazing mess, at least by Mom's standards. She was obviously desperate to go out of town. There had been a long discussion the last time Dad had tried to leave me with Richard for a weekend. This was the life. A new Asteroids personal high score too, it took me three hours. They would never let me do that at home.

The rest of it is a blur, really. The crowd, eighties Long Island, mainly metal, but mostly just kind of rough and messy. Not like a hockey or basketball crowd: this was my first time to the Coliseum for a show. People were definitely getting messed up and I had to be high just from all the smoke. I wished my denim jacket was a little more beat up, that I looked a bit tougher. I don't know, I felt like the youngest person there, but I felt safe too—Richard was from a different, non-parental kind of space, but he kept an eye on me, all three of them did.

It was so loud. I did not know things could be so loud. And the crowd response was incredible, singing along and screaming. Overwhelming. The lights.

And then it happened. They started "Highway to Hell;" the lights went up, the crowd delirious. There was a beautiful woman standing next to me. In a year or two I would not have been able to take my eyes off her. She took a hit off a joint, turned to me and smiled, and passed it to me. She was hot and I basked in the glow of that smile.

I reached out to take the joint.

Richard leaned in and beat me to it.

"Not yet kid, not on my watch," he said. He smiled too, he wasn't mad.

Corny remembered where he was, and for a moment felt everything that had passed in the times since then. So many choices, so many changes. Too many regrets and lots of laughs. He was pretty sure knowing what he did now probably would not have made much of a difference.

Then he thought of Cissy, his perfect niece, and how she was not going to be a kid for that much longer. Maybe he'd give them a call next time he was in cell range—perhaps Friday in Belturbet. She definitely needs to be listening to better music. What are her parents up to?

Meanwhile, his feet and legs were soaked and cold and he couldn't take the old rock anymore. He ditched the headphones and listened to the wind and the rain and the squish in his shoes. From a peaceful and quiet night he now felt lonely, small, and old. Cold legs and cold feet.

His whimsy gone, he marched into the night.

CORNELIUS AND LUCILLE
AT THE GROCERY STORE — II

Corny looks at every face like he's going to know them, have a laugh to exchange.

He had crashed at Lucille's on return. He had spent a few days here and there driving—down to Oly, Centralia even, up to Mountlake Terrace, Whidbey. Not much success, but some old connections starting to heat up.

Things were starting to get tight. It looked like the virus would be shutting everything down soon. He had checked on his place in Columbia City. His tenants there had a lease through June. He wasn't sure about what to do. Where would he be at the end of June?

Lucille let him stay in the backyard garage/guesthouse. A little bit of cleaning, a new futon, and it was ready to go.

In terms of sustenance, they had both been living on a steady diet of take-out over the two weeks since getting to town. Not much cooking or shopping had gone on. Looking at the coming hurry up and wait scenario, considering how it would complicate their hunt for Lulu, a need to stock up had been arrived and agreed upon.

"The lack of mustard would not be so crushing, but there's no mayo, no ketchup, no Cholula, no Sriracha. It is time to shop."

Normally, coming to this awareness on a Sunday night would not be too much of an issue, but it was the last night of February and the first fatality had been announced this afternoon. They heard it while driving back to Seattle. They had been making jokes about the guy in Coupeville who had given Corny the number of a woman he called "Love" in Seattle who might know where some of the people he hoped to talk to were.

It was going to be a big shop. Condiment deep.

They had not considered a bunch of panic buying in relation to the virus news. But the parking lot was packed—period—not just for this time of night. There were lines at the registers.

"People sure seem uptight. So quiet, despite the crowd."

There was plenty of coffee though; same with produce.

"The broccoli is amazing. The broccoli I could get in Cavan was not like this. And avocados. It was like I'd buy myself an avocado on my birthday. I'd go all the way to Dublin to get one."

Everything was in order until they got to the bulk section, which had been totally cleaned out. They were lucky to get a big bag of arborio and the last of the oats. Pickles and sauerkraut; acquired. The olive bar was devastated, no muffeletta or any kalamatas in sight. They were pleased to have not had toilet paper on their list, because there wasn't sign of any on the shelves.

The shelves were sparse in areas, full in others. Plenty of great cheese to be had: goat, brie, bleu, but no cheddar or parmesan to be found. Not even romano. No feta either. There was a full selection of condiments to refresh the bare kitchen, lots of beer and ice cream too. Certain needs tend to be easy to meet. The same was not true for eggs and half and half, the dairy section had been ravaged. Some strange yogurt and vegan cream cheese were all that remained. There was some tofu, but only silken.

"It is going to be strange sitting around."

"Or potentially weird to move around. Imagine everything locked down but we're driving around on the wild Lulu chase."

"What does Love like to eat?"

"Am I going to have to share a meal with her? I'll talk to her if she gets me on Lulu's trail. Or whoever has her. I have a hard time believing that, though perhaps Lulu attracted the wrong attention."

"Not the first time."

"Nor the last." It felt strange to put it that way, an unwanted possibility, one he prefer remain weightless. "Whatever."

The bread selection was forlorn, but that was to be expected late on a Sunday evening. Despite the purpose of their trip, to fill a bare kitchen, they did not avoid the deli and all its temptation. Corny waxed at great length about the amazing mac and cheese as opposed to Ireland. He talked about it a long time. He really liked mac and cheese. When they had flown back into town he had made her stop at Beecher's in the airport for the mac and cheese. By far his most unreasonable moment since he had left his Irish homestead.

"Take that Ezra. Always going on about your mac and cheese. Lucille, I'd make you some great mac and cheese, but it will have to wait."

"Right. There might not be any pasta in a ten-mile radius. Who knew there was such a thing as gourmet mac and cheese?"

Corny rolled his eyes, pretended she had stabbed him in the heart.

"Tough for you—you'll have my risotto before you get my mac and cheese."

"You can work with that, *arborio*?"

"I will," he promised.

Things were light. They were almost done. They laughed at the crazy panic buying, like the night before a snowstorm. People, you love people, but you seem to feel better when they aren't around.

Lucille took a breath in shock, "we almost forgot to get peanut butter."

"Must have peanut butter."

They were shocked when they got to where the peanut butter should have been. The stampede had obviously been here. No, there was no super-sized jar of crunchy organic. There were some small jars of almond butter that had big prices.

Lucille's mood had palpably dampened. Then she found a jar, a small one, at the back of the shelf hiding in shadow. A lonely portent of the time at hand and the time to come.

"It's small, it's smooth, it's sweetened," she cried as she looked at the label.

This information seemed to stop Corny as well. He fussed and fretted in disbelief, he caught himself starting to mutter about the apocalypse and Love. He stopped, catching himself, and seemed to raise himself up.

"Wow," he said, "shit is getting real."

CORNELIUS SWIMS TO THE SWIZZLE STICK — III

"You were connected to this boat, this guy, by a woman named Love?"

They had been going over their plan for days. The plan was not complicated, but it had been set out. He had not let the love part slip until now. Unnecessary background information, silly to share it now..

"Love? Shit. At every turn this just gets weirder."

"Look, I don't know her. I know someone who knows her. Lulu really does run with the kind of folks that you, that you might not see in a general sample of your fellow citizens."

"It's just so…"

"Ridiculous, I know. But look at us, look at me. How ridiculous is all of this?"

He watched her assessing him. While he did not normally see himself as someone who might dazzle while wearing a nice tight wetsuit out for the evening, the night, the bay, the more-than-mist but less-than-drizzle and yet somehow continuous precipitation had rendered him more than usually un-self-conscious. His tuber-shaped shadow caught in the iPhone flashlight did not make his spirits any more moist than they already were.

"Is her name really Love?"

"Yes. As I said, I do not know much about her. Much at all. But she's our connection here. Last I looked we don't have many choices. And while she is likely a bit unusual, even for my tastes, she's our connection and I do not have the luxury of caring about what her name is."

"I know. Crazy as all this is, her name makes it all funnier and sadder and more twisted all at once. These days, everything seems like a backward omen."

"You are telling me. And mind you, I am a bit sensitive about names. Be superstitious if you want—it makes a certain amount of sense. But what else are we going to do?"

Cornelius and Lucille stood on the shore of Lake Washington, Bailey's Bay, the last night of March in the year of the pandemic. Our man, clad in a wetsuit—a thick one, about to swim out to a boat anchored in the middle of the bay. All in a quest to get some more information about the whereabouts of Lulu.

Corny had had to dredge up old connections, all as the world shut down. Eventually there had been notes, and a couple of meetings, with masks and social distance. All leading to swimming to a boat in the middle of the bay on a late winter-early spring night.

"Now that I think of it," said Corny, "at least I've been close to Love, even if I couldn't see her face, even if she was just out of reach."

Lucille's eye roll could be seen in the dark.

"At least we don't know the name of the guy on the boat—knowledge can hurt. Be careful what you ask for. I am looking for a small boat, named "Swizzle Stick," and it is not the biggest boat in the bay, it is one of the other two. No devices—nothing signal capable. There's plenty to feel ridiculous about."

He turned, so she could see his profile in the shadow of the phone's light, theatrically presenting himself.

"Just don't call me Mr. Potato Head—it's the kind of thing that happens to me all the time when I go out dressed like this."

He turned to face her, she forced a thin smile, and he backed slowly into the water. The water was cold and the suit was very thick. No cramps though. He got out to where it was deep enough to float. His first attempt at "see you soon" came out as a croak from his chilly constricted lungs.

Love had said no digital communication; and when he came out to the boat he could not use a boat of his own, he would have to swim. Corny still hadn't wrapped his head around that part. Don't bring any devices with you. There's a fine line between being curious and being realistic: other options had not been located.

He had come to interact with his curiosity differently, because the rules that seemed to operate were generally not coherent. Fly back to the states at the start of a pandemic to search for his for-mer—what—lover? Partner in crime? Madness-inducing friend? Greatest embarrasser? Part of him wanted to say abuser at first, but that was the part of him that had once expected different things, as well as an admission to a repeatedly trampled-upon heart. And abuse wasn't the right word anyway.

He asked himself why these things played out this way. He hadn't gotten any answers; no satisfying, repeatable assessments. Just repeated violations of what he had been taught to expect. So, he stopped expecting those things. He grew so comfortable with eccentricity, he worried that he did not stop to ask the appropriate questions anymore. Like, why? Why are you doing this?

Why? Because a string of information, initiated, at least in part, by people whom he trusted, had led him here. Because he no longer knew what else to do. Something about the stream of his life and the course of events he observed seemed to carry him to right now. Maybe someone would finally pull back the curtain and say it had all been a joke, and then he would have to take it like a gut punch cry and sob because he had fallen for it.

But for now, so what?

The water wasn't inky or black. It struck him as thin, un-supporting. The water held him up, barely, and the cold lurked, tentacles reaching, draining his heat as it became available. His brain was almost not anywhere else.

Lulu wasn't on his mind.

The virus wasn't on his mind.

The (it should be assumed) scary character on the boat wasn't on his mind.

He wished the night was clear, so he could look to Orion and Venus from his back in the bay. The waxing gibbous moon occasionally appeared through the moving clouds.

He thought about Lucille. He wondered how his bitcoin shares were doing. It had been a rocky month.

He lay on his back, conserving energy, and slowly paddled toward the shadow he thought was the Swizzle Stick. He could not remember the last time he had swum in open water, let alone a couple of hundred yards on a cold night.

II

No, don't say that, he told himself. Saying that is like saying you want to fight about it, or at least you are ready to and willing to debate.

No, just eat that memo. Destroy the evidence. File it away, because if you think about it you are going to talk about it. He already felt like he was holding his breath.

"He really introduced himself as Colonel Mustard?"

"Yes Lucille, he did. He really did. Then he sighed, said don't worry about it, that I could call him Gary."

He giggled despite the shivering and his still blue lips. Lucille smirked.

"Did he have a silly hat on?"

"Not really, an ancient Mariners hat: one with a trident."

"So, did you two talk about how the virus is ruining your sports life?"

"No baseball talk on the Swizzle Stick tonight. Just a little bit of business"

This Colonel Gary Mustard did not really have any information. Or a knack for pretending he was someone other than he was.

"Did Gary do this willingly? Someone making him, sounds like it?"

"He certainly seemed lukewarm on the whole thing. Or more like he thought it could be fun but then he thought it was all stupid. He was disappointed that his conditions and the swim didn't nearly kill me or piss me off. A little bit like if this guy thinks this is standard business I am not going to play."

"Well, you did get to talk to Love."

"Love, oh love. Who knows, someone wants us mystified, confused, this Gary wants, or whoever put him up to this wants, something, wants us to do something."

She looked at him. Waiting. She knew if it took prying it probably wasn't something to be happy about.

Corny pulled the blanket tighter around him. He wished it all made more sense. But don't we all.

"Well," he shivered, "the directions are simple. They want some stuff of Lulu's and they think we—I—can find it. He would not tell me why Lulu could not just give him the directions. He smiled when I asked, and said, 'I think you understand what this is about'."

"So?" guessed Lucille, "they want her rocks."

"Her 'gems' was how Gary put it."

"Simple, but how? Where?"

"Well, he said they maybe could be a little patient because everything is shut down. But not too patient. He also said Lulu was safe, like we didn't know that."

"Right. They need her. But where is our incentive? Beyond how stuck we are in this loop."

"I think Gary, or whoever sent him, assumes we're in."

"So, what's next?"

"Well," Corny winced, "it involves a storage locker in Sea-Tac."

CLARK HUMPHREY

Clark Humphrey has seen Seattle transform from a boom-and-bust industrial city into today's fast-growing, fast-moving tech and corporate Mecca (albeit slowed down by the events of 2020). His books include LOSER: The Real Seattle Music Story *(reissued by MISCmedia),* Walking Seattle *(from Wilderness Press), and* Vanishing Seattle *and* Seattle's Belltown *(both from Arcadia Publishing). He writes daily about the city, its growth, and its contradictions at miscmedia.com.*

ASIDE FROM THAT, THEY NEVER TOUCHED

Part I

She had her arms around his leather jacket as she rode on the back of his Harley. Aside from that, they never touched.

Greta wore enough of a coat herself that there was nothing more than a slight breast bump against his back. Still, she knew that it usually took very little to get some guys turned on, and who knew what this guy would end up doing if he decided there was no downside to assaulting her?

Especially at some of the places he was driving her past. Places that would seem lonesome during the day, but were downright scary-creepy at night. Especially at night during the Distancing, with most things closed and few cars and fewer people around. Just the streets, the parking lots, and the structures. The steel mill; the concrete plant with its concrete dome; the giant Lego stacks of cargo containers; and the reproduction Native long-house on the other side of the street. At almost any of the places they passed, he could have thrown her off the bike, stopped it at a spot that would make her escape difficult, and forced himself on/in her. Each moment he didn't do any of that simply increased her apprehension that he still could.

Along the way, Greta yelled to him what she'd been doing when she'd met him. She never knew whether he really heard, under his helmet, any of what she yelled. About dropping off her broken Samsung phone at the closest independent repair shop still open. About neglecting to call for an Uber from the repair shop. About learning the hard way the bus route she needed to get home was on reduced service. About trying to find the next closest street that still had buses running, when he drove up beside her at the dark quiet bus stop, with some other bikers in the distance with their backs to her, talking quietly and seriously among themselves.

Why did she keep talking, when he probably wouldn't listen even if he could? It later became obvious: she was talking to drown out her own fear from her own mind. And she was talking on the slight chance that if she managed to even slightly human-ize herself in his eyes, he'd be just a slight chance less likely to shoot her or stab her, even if he did assault her first.

But he stayed on the handlebars, on the road, down West Marginal and then Highway 99, across the South Park bridge, and eventually onto north Beacon Hill and her house. He didn't take his hands off the handlebars when she offered to shake his hand. He didn't raise his helmet's visor when he said goodnight. He just drove into the distance, one loud Hog disrupting, then disappearing into, an eerily silent residential street.

Months later, she learned what his real plans for her had been, and that his plans had worked. She was unable to positively identify any of the other bikers, the ones who'd been involved in the robbery at the place she'd been driven away from. She didn't even reliably remember what she'd seen of her driver's face, in the dark before his stuck his helmet on.

And the roundabout way she drove her home? It was to first get her far away from the bus stop in front of the robbery site, then to keep her away from it.

The day after the ride, her two best friends suggested in a video chat that she might have secretly wanted him to seduce her, to initiate her into his world of dark danger, and she's probably still in denial about wanting it/him. She scoffed out loud at the very notion. Really!

Part II

The best part of Greta's day used to be sharing wine, chips, and salsa after work with "the girls." Now it's the same thing, in Zoom form. The only times this doesn't happen are when one of the three has to work late. Unfortunately, that's been happening a lot more often the past week or two (as if weeks and days mattered right now).

So when all three finally got virtually together for the first time in five days, she had a lot to tell them.

And she knew that what she most needed to tell them about was what they most wanted to learn about: her new life with the biker guy she'd met when he gave her a ride home that night, and whom she'd re-met when he was acquitted of abetting a burglary ring.

Before she logged on, her two "baes" Stef and Cara chatted among themselves. They took bets on whether she'd show up on camera with big frizzed hair and an online-bought biker jacket, maybe even a Harley logo tank top and fake tattoos (until she can get real ones). They agreed she must have instantly become a biker chick—just like she'd transformed over the years, in the presence of previous boyfriends, into an instant soccer geek, an instant wine snob, and an instant jazz historian.

The two women lost their mutual bets when she popped up on their computer screens looking exactly like her self, only with five more days' worth of hair in the same style.

As usual, Stef and Cara teased Greta about becoming a motorcycle mama, learning to ride a Hog and carry a switchblade, practicing for the wet T-shirt contest at Sturgis.

Nope. None of that. She was still working remotely in the legal department, still crunching numbers and Zoom-chatting about contracts and liabilities.

The biker: Oh, he was still around. It wasn't like he could easily move out or anything.

But he was turning himself into her clone.

He was taking an online coding course.

He was online-buying office casual clothes, asking her advice on the best color schemes for him.

He was listening to her classic vocal-jazz CDs, learning to appreciate Ella and Billie (though he still preferred Sinatra).

He was trying to become the perfect boyfriend—which, according to some online articles he'd found, involved cooking and cleaning without her asking him to, as well as letting her "take the lead" in bed.

The last she looked before logging into this chat, he'd been reading up about how to cut his own hair.

Her loyal (if sometimes impossible) best friends had a quick diagnosis.

He, they surmised, was trying to quickly integrate himself deeply into her life.

He was trying to become such a normal, everyday part of her existence that by the time she can kick him out she won't. He'll be part of the furniture, albeit a part of the furniture that's learned how to get her off every time.

Greta hated it when Stef and Cara barbed her with sexual taunts. They knew she hated it. They regularly did it anyway, like grade-school girls who knew just how angry they could make each other get without it hurting.

Greta was still formulating a wicked response, something along the lines of "at least I've got a real man in my house, not just a piece of plastic with batteries," when she heard a noise from the living room. Before she could stand up, he'd trotted into the dining nook that had become her home office, holding out his smartphone, asking what she thought of these Oxford shoes he was thinking of getting.

SNEAKING HER IN

Part I

Embarking on global voyages; fighting and killing; making impossible promises; making complete embarrassing asses of themselves; falling down from ladders or out of suddenly unparked cars. From experience, history, literature, tales told by friends and ex-lovers, and most of the bad comedy movies of the 1980s and '90s, Jerry knew about the many crazy things guys have done to get laid.

A world whose history didn't include guys being led around by their unreliable organs would be a quiet world indeed, Jerry thought. Almost as quiet as the world surrounding his place this afternoon.

Jerry had already decided it would be unnecessarily creepy to buy a bunch of webcams online, get them delivered, and install them surreptitiously at all the approaches to his place. Besides, he probably couldn't get them delivered in time. And he wasn't enough of a hardware nerd to correctly install them.

So he texted Litsa some instructions on the day of the meeting, instructions as specific as he could make them. Show up at a specific time, arriving from a specific direction. Make sure nobody else is approaching the place. If possible, make sure nobody else is around to see her.

She went along with everything he asked, with a smiley emoji in her response. Apparently she figured it was some role playing fantasy of his. He texted her that he wouldn't do this for anyone except her; that she was special to him. Litsa texted back that he probably texted that to all the girls.

As he'd instructed, Litsa texted him as soon as she was within a block of his place. He watched from a slightly opened stairwell door to make sure it was clear. No mailmen or women. No deliveries. Nobody hanging out downstairs. He quickly darted out toward the front door just as she approached it.

Jerry mildly exhorted her to hurry up and get inside. She giggled. "Aren't you a little old to be sneaking girls up into your room? Is your mommy about to come home and catch us?"

As he led her into the seldom-used stairwell up to his place, Litsa barely caught a glimpse of the printout sign, in small type, taped to a wall in the building lobby, with the bold-faced headline: "DURING COVID-19 RESTRICTIONS, NO VISITORS OR GUESTS ALLOWED IN BUILDING."

Part II

Jerry awoke smiling, content, clear. It had been weeks since he'd gotten a full night's sleep, without either staying in bed worrying about nothing in particular or getting up watching nothing in particular online.

It was also weeks, months, since he'd had non-solo sex. Since he'd felt the touch of skin other than his own. Since he'd had another person's breaths, another person's smells, near him.

And now it was morning. The lark of bad news on cable news channels, not the nightingale of Litsa's cooing and mumbling and moaning. Only he had no desire to turn on any electronics, not while the auto-repeat audio program from Litsa's phone was still quietly humming its reassuring ambient synth tones from the bedside dresser top.

He looked up and saw Litsa was still there. Of course she was. He'd warned her not to wander out into the corridor while other residents might hear her, report him to the manager, and get him kicked out of the building (once it became legal to kick residents out of apartments again).

He kissed her awake. She smiled.

She reached across him to the dresser, giving him a good view of her mature but still-trim torso. If he'd had the energy, he'd have grabbed hold of her. Instead, he just let her move.

He asked her about the audio track. She said she could email him a copy. He said he'd prefer to hear it with her voice at the same time. She smiled and kissed him warmly as she retrieved the phone and stood up. She said that could be arranged; though preferably at her place, where there wasn't a no-guests-or-visitors policy. She said he could think about it while she showered and dressed.

She took the phone into the front area of the studio apartment. Before she set it into her purse, she thought of how she'd prepared the audio. It did have her voice on it, in deep background, relating a hypnotic narrative:

"You are in a beautiful place. A peaceful place. All the cares and problems of the outside world are truly far away here. As you breathe in the healthy clean air, your body radiates healthy warmth. A slight warm breeze assures you: you are where you were always meant to be. You hear a voice. It is the voice of the one you love. You know you are safe; you know you are cared for. Your body feels one primary sensation. It is the magic metal band around your finger. You know it will protect you. The words on on the band promise this. The words are etched in a perfect, elegant script: Litsa and Jerry, Now and Forever."

EXCERPTS FROM
OTHELLO PLACE:
A TALE OF FAMILY AND DESTINY
IN MODERN AMERICA
(A SCRIPT TREATMENT FOR
A NEVER-TO-BE-PRODUCED TV SERIES)

PART I:
DRED'S PARENTS CUT EXPENSES

(MILDRED "DRED" CANARY is in her family home. She's on the phone with her best fried DARA "DAR" VIGIL. She's speaking softly, to avoid being heard by her parents.)

DRED: So the thing is, we've had food from their cafe for dinner at least two days a week for the past month.

DAR: From your parents' cafe?

DRED: Yeah. I mean, it's good stuff and all that. You know.

DAR: But I thought the Othello Place Cafe was still closed.

DRED: Except for take out, yeah. But they've been bringing some of the stuff home. The sandwich meats, the breads, the condiments, the pasta and sauce, the burger patties. My mom and dad try to fix them up different every time. Different seasonings, sauces, combinations, toppings, ways of cooking.

DAR: Are they test driving new things to put on the menu when they're completely open again?

DRED: That's what they're telling me. But I have my doubts.

DAR: I know you. You probably have your own idea of what's really going on. (A small gasp.) Oh: you think they're trying to eat up the stock before it spoils?

DRED: If it was just that, they could just donate it to the food banks. They always used to do that.

DAR: Oh no. Do you really think they're...

DRED: Trying to save money, yeah.

DAR: Like how serious? 'Let's be a little stingy for a couple of weeks so we can pay back the IRS' serious, or 'choose just your best clothes, we're moving into the car' serious?

DRED: More like the first than the second. I hope. But it's hard to tell.

DAR: How?

DRED: Just the way they've been acting. You know the way parents act when they don't tell you anything, or they insist everything's just normal, well as normal as things can be these days anyway?

DAR: Yeah? You're saying that's what they're doing?

DRED: Sort of. I guess. I mean, they admit times are tough with almost no money coming in, and that troll of a landlord acting all giddy at the thought of being able to evict the cafe as soon as the state will let him with this official eviction ban and all that. They had to lay off Treez's mom. They applied for a small business grant lottery; didn't win.

DAR: So what do you think will happen?

DRED: I know my dad in particular would rather do almost anything than let that landlord Benny get to kick out the cafe.

DAR: But what will they do? I mean, what can they do?

DRED: I'm only guessing, but maybe give up the house and move us into the storage room?

DAR: But hey: at least you've found a way to make them stay together. I mean, before all this virus stuff went down, that's what you cared about the most, right?

DRED: Yeah for now, I guess, we're still a 'family unit.' If they do lose the cafe, they could lose any reason to stick together. My dad could go back to seeing Shawn's mom, and my mom could shack up with that artist guy Otis.

DAR: And where would YOU go?

DRED: I don't want to think about that. I just want to deal with one dreadful crisis at a time. As much as I can.

PART 2:
DAR AND DRED VS. ONLINE MATH CLASS

(DAR and DRED are on a two way video Skype call from their respective bedrooms. They're bored out of their (not as mature as they think they are) skulls.)

DAR: I'm bored out of my skull!

DRED: I'm more bored than you are.

DAR: No, that's just not possible. Nobody on earth could be as totally, utterly, completely B-O-R-E-D as I am right now.

DRED: I know: let's call a truce. Let's agree we're both bored with the whole restriction quarantine online-school online-everything situation.

DAR: You said it, girlfriend. On the one hand, everything we hated about school—everything that wasn't directly learning stuff—it's all gone in online school.

DRED: On the other hand, it turns out that what we both used to hate was really what got us through the day there. Without all the girls to sneer at behind their backs, without all the guys to sneer at straight to their faces, without all the usual things they did to survive the day, all that's left of school is, well, "school." The thing itself.

DAR: And, when it's not a break from everything that doesn't make sense, what does make sense makes really grim sense.

DRED: Yeah, Ms. Chiang in math class says it's preparation for our futures. But it's preparation for a really boring future. A future where everybody's stuck at computer screens all day just like now, but going on forever, or at least until death, and the tech bros with their "biohacking" nonsense are trying to even prevent that from ever happening.

DAR: But math.

DRED: Yeah math.

DAR: Apparently back in my father's time, math was something where you had to learn enough of it to pass the test and would never need to remember most of it again. But now, school administrators all over the world have decided together that everybody has to love math, because everybody has to become a programmer. Everybody's supposed to want to be a total tech bro.

DRED: Especially all the girls. They made us watch that "Hidden Figures" movie. They tell us how the great scientific breakthroughs were really the work of low-paid women and college girls sitting at mechanical calculators all day.

DAR: Well, that's because girls have always been great at doing all the real work that just has to get done, while the guys strut around telling each other dumb jokes and boasting about how wonderful they are.

DRED: So anyway: Math. And online math class. With these dumb games where you have to use math to figure out the answer.

DAR: And puzzles to solve, because we're not supposed to be interested in the real work without some game part of it to keep us alert.

DRED: And then there was this whole video we had to watch about how there's math everywhere in the world. Like DUH.

DAR: We already know there's math in music. My dad being a jazz guy, and you in your Rock Girls Camp. And my nana's old recipes are full of numbers.

DRED: So what would your nana say about these dumb games and puzzles?

DAR: She'd probably say that's just more of what you have to go through, to get to what you really have to go through.

(DRED silently nods.)

PART 3:
CHRISTY AND GORDON TALK ABOUT DRED

The Canary family has finished dinner. In the family kitchen, CHRISTY receives a cell phone call. After listening for a few seconds, CHRISTY gives a hand signal to GORDON. GORDON, then, verbally calls for his and Christy's daughter Dred to finish her desert upstairs in her room and then get back to her online homework. DRED, knowing that it's a call she's not supposed to hear, gives a polite "excuse me please" to her parents and leaves the room with her cake, but not before cutting herself a second slice.

Once DRED is safely out of the room, CHRISTY puts the phone

call on speaker mode. It's HANNAH, the mother of DRED's best friend DAR. She's got a word of warning to CHRISTY and GORDON about their daughter: "Your MILDRED and my DARA seem to have been involved in some nefarious shenanigans." HANNAH tells about the trip DAR had taken to BENNY's real estate office, about the attempt to hide microphones all over the Vigil house. Oh, and there was also the little matter of the bugging of DAR's father's cell phone.

From her room, where she's got big ass headphones on, DRED listens in on the phone call from downstairs via CHRISTY's bugged phone, and realizes the jig is up. There's only one thing she can do at this point: eat more cake.

But then, HANNAH assures CHRISTY that bugging your family's cell phones is something DARA did, but probably not something MILDRED would do, because MILDRED seems to trust her parents a little more. In the Canary kitchen, CHRISTY pretends to agree; GORDON nonverbally expresses his doubts. From her room listening in, DRED breathes a sigh of at least temporary relief.

HANNAH and CHRISTY talk about how DAR and DRED are control freaks. CHRISTY opines that, while other teens are big on trying to generate chaos, in the world around them and in their own lives, DAR and DRED try to stay in control of their own lives and to get control of the world around them. One aspect of that, HANNAH brings up, is that neither of the girls is all that keen on dating, or on expressions of sexuality of any kind.

CHRISTY opens up about how when she was DRED's age, she was always running around trying to remove the pants from any guy her age who didn't seem like a potential serial killer. HANNAH says she was never "that wild" at that point of her life, due to her church upbringing; "but when I got out of the house and off to college, "there were a lot of nice Christian young men who needed to receive the Good News about my body." But CHRISTY notes that MILDRED, and DARA too, only talk about boys when they're talking about how much fun it is to insult them.

In her room listening in on the phone call, DRED says to herself, "What else do you expect me to do with guys? No, mom, don't go there. No, self, don't even think about going there."

After the phone call with HANNAH has ended, CHRISTY and GORDON talk about their daughter. GORDON quips that it's at least a nice break from talking about money trouble and their mostly-closed cafe. CHRISTY doesn't diss the joke, but simply says those problems, however difficult they are right now, are temporary. We WILL get over it. MILDRED's development as a young woman, however: That's something major. That's something long-term. That's something that will affect the rest of your life. GORDON says DRED's been behaving a lot more maturely than he ever did when he was her age, and he turned out OK. Well, sort of, at least. CHRISTY jokingly asks GORDON not to give her any more reminders of why they're separating. GORDON briefly laughs out loud.

From upstairs in her room, now with the big ass headphones off, DRED strains to hear what her parents are saying down in the kitchen. All she can really discern are a few brief snitches of words and GORDON's occasional bouts of out-loud laughter.

The following day, CHRISTY and GORDON are again talking about their daughter DRED, now from inside the kitchen at the closed-except-for-takeout Othello Place Cafe. The physical "business" in this scene, and the official reason why they're both on the premises this day when there's typically been not even enough take out business for one person to handle: taking inventory of food items that need to be used, tossed, or donated; making an online order to the food suppliers based on their currently way-reduced needs.

CHRISTY : "Up to this point, we've been glad that DRED has been a little difficult to deal with and to talk with, a little attitude prone, but a girl who always stayed out of any real trouble. And, yes, a girl whose attitude toward boys, and toward that whole aspect of life, has remained like that of a fifth grade girl perpetually sticking her tongue out at those gross immature boys. But…" GORDON gives a call-and-response reply: "But what?" CHRISTY tells GORDON it's a good thing they're splitting up, since now that means she doesn't care any more about GORDON's dumb buttinsky remarks.

CHRISTY continues: "But what if she should be moving on from that phase by now? What if, instead of her lording it over the other girls from school as the ultimate gossip queen, they decide she's just a trashy little girl in a teenager's body? What if boys, or or that matter girls if she turns out to be 'that way,' just up and decide she's more trouble than she's worth? That kind of universal rejection could just emotionally scar someone for life."

GORDON tells CHRISTY, "Not to worry, not to worry. Different kids mature in different stages at different times. DRED started walking when it was time for her. She started talking when it was time for her. She started dressing herself when it was time for her. She'll know for herself when it's time for her to ride the emotional roller coaster of young romance. To be all crushed and disappointed when the first guy she tries to sleep with mistakenly thinks sex in real life is like the sex in the pornos. To have some clingy geeky guy be madly, sadly, obsessively in love with her, when all she wants to do is run as far away from him as possible.

CHRISTY interrupts this rant to note that all these imaginary teenage boys GORDON is describing sound a lot like the kind of teenage boy he himself might have been. GORDON responds with a loud laugh and a hearty "No comment."

JOANNE KLEIN

I've been singing since age 4. I've been acting as an amateur since age 25, professionally since age 33. Teaching and coaching actors and singers since age 51. Writing actual stories at age 68. Wrote the play Bloody Saddles *at age 35, never produced. Wrote (with five other women) the play* Pants on Fire, *produced at the Empty Space Theatre, at age 46. Adapted* Alice in Wonderland *for StageStruck Musical Theatre Camp age 57. Wrote and produced a whole bunch of cabaret shows, including* Are My Themes Straight *and* Hagapalooza, *from age 40 to now. Singing jazz for the last twenty-something years. Now that I look back and see my resume, I've been busy, that is rather successful. I'd be contented except art is so much fun to continue. Art outlives politics. Art saves lives. I also love chocolate. Ironically, I love ironing.*

ALKI ALONE

Okay, she has her phone, ID, pills, hankie and little Phillips head screwdriver... ready. Lately she's been taking it along since she's getting a feeling, a sense of more "crazy-ness" in the air then there used to be. She is devoted to walking down by Alki. But then, they did find those two suitcases with the body parts over by Salty's, so... look what that got them. Creepy. But those folks weren't from around here, still, crazy.

A while ago, probably years now, she'd found the quieter side on Beach Drive over where the brass octopus is embedded in the sidewalk. The street's been closed off now for the plague, and it's less traveled than before. It's great! She loves walking on the Constellation sidewalk on the leeward side. And just strolling on the actual street is like being little again, in the neighborhoods way back when cars had to look out for all the kids, so it felt oddly safe. Now, neighbor kids are using the street as a chalk canvas. And in case the times get unusual, her little screwdriver makes her feel she could have a fighting chance, but nobody is down here at ten pm, it's closed up. The people who are floating around are going home or walking the dog or just out by the beach.

She breathes so many deep breaths, oh this sea air. She feels her whole body relax, and looks at the lights on the islands and wonders why more people aren't down here? Oh, right, it's Seattle. It's a morning town so she has the evening to herself. Doesn't need a mask, has one. It's so quiet. Heading windward past the lighthouse her pace becomes a little quicker. She passes her favorite house with the black and white striped awning and fig color paint job, and the blue-lights house, and the long beach, and as she nears the commercial area which is usually busy with cruising cars, it's quiet and even though there's only a few people around, she decides to head back. She thinks lots of people are afraid of the night. There's still twenty-four hours! But the seasons have changed, and the calm of the summer drifting into the drafty fall does feel spookier. That long darkness that starts at four p.m. And no sun until seven a.m. But tonight, the sky is clear. And stars are everywhere. And it's still and peaceful. And she hopes it will always feel safe enough.

CHARLIE AND V8
(A ME TOO PIPEDREAM)

I was blabbing to my stepdaughter Leah last week. We try to catch up when we can but she, her sister Rachel and I are busy, and its weeks before we can get together, so this was great. We were at the Mosaic, this old bar and grill with mosaics everywhere. She was filling me in on all the epic gossip around her family and I was going on about the general nonsense in my life. And then she said, "You know, I am sane because of you..." I'm like, "What?" And she's fast; "Yeah, I know my parents love us and they are ridiculous and crazy and smart, but you were the one who tracked my sanity!"

Of course, my heart is beaming with pride and joy, that I am positively influencing anyone, but this was slightly different... "Oh? Why's that?"

"Remember that story you told us about when you were around nineteen, twenty?"

"Uhhhh, which one?" I ask.

"The one about the toad?!"

"Oh... oh, yeah, yes of course..."

"And do you remember your advice about sex?" she asked.

"Wow Leah, when didn't I mouth off about that?"

"Well, alright, the one about walking into a bar and picking out who you were going to have sex with...how you didn't care, you just ..."

"Yes..." I interrupted her and reeling back to those days, when I would walk into a bar, any cool bar, look around and think, "I'd fuck him, I wouldn't fuck him, I'd fuck her, I wouldn't fuck her, I'd fuck him, or him or him or her, or No I wouldn't fuck him... "Okay, witty, true, very horny... so what about that kept you sane?"

"Well, you said it was a safer time, all those diseases you could cure... but it was what you said after, about being sober first. About looking a man in the eyes and seeing them, seeing you, looking for someone who wasn't so drunk or so insane, or nuts, and seeing someone who was nice, potentially a sort of Mr. Right?"

I remembered how somewhere in my twenties I realized I was Mr. Right.

"…And you were lucky."

"Yep, almost all the time!" I stopped thinking about my past. I asked "Okay, what about the toad?" I'm thinking, "where is she going with this?"

"You remember how you said when you were still living on the east coast, that this guy said he could help your performing career get off the ground, but that you would have to have sex with him?"

"Yeah, yes."

"And you told him that wasn't going to happen, and he said well he didn't think you'd have much of a career because this was going to happen again, 'cause you're such a cutie pie…"

Wow, way back there again. How was I so, what? Intuitive? To not call him a toad, to tell him "I think I'll try it my way first and if I ever need to sleep with you, I'll get back to you" And I walked out the door… "So, Leah, what is going on?"

"You are not going to believe this, but I got a call from Charlie Rose!!"

"Whaaattt!" "No Way!!" "What?!?!"

"Yep… he called me! Well, someone from his entourage emailed first to say that Mr. Rose would be calling and here's the number to expect. Because I wrote him to give him a piece of advice."

"No, Wow, what happened? I am so disappointed in him."

"Yeah, I know. I'm online and it turns out he is investigating all sorts of women or people and hunting, really, he typed hunting, for something that will make him feel better or some such crap, and I wrote him about Your Stories. There was an email to respond to, and a phone number to leave a message rather than write, and he called. He thought your tales were funny and real, so, he called to ask why I wrote to him. I told him I hadn't had as much experience as my stepmom, but because of her, I was safe. And not about to be taken advantage of because I had really thought about what sex meant to me. Again, I am talking to Charlie Rose. He laughed a few times and kind of interrupted me with "That's true, or Uh huhs and I just kept plowing away. I just kept thinking what would you say!"

"And!"

"And I told him that his legacy was forever tarnished, forever. Any women or man who is really kind, sane, good, and loves sex, not power but honest, altruistic, humane, powerfully fucking good time, and oh, yeah, collaborative, knows that power is something to be distributed with wisdom and care, like Solomon, or Brecht's Azdak or Jimmy Fucking Carter, and Mr. Rogers, you know, great goodness, Mr. Rose. Not clandestine prurient, coy, boyish retardation, and with any luck you will never be famous again for your great mind but for your infamy. Those of us who like, love sex don't use it against someone else like a thug, or with lies or cheating or sado-masochistic narcissistic play acting."

"AND"

"And there was this long silence and finally, I figured he'd hung up but just as I was about to say Mr. Rose, he said, "I coulda had a V8?"

I laughed. Like a spit take. Like milk coming out of my nose.

Leah had to think about this. V8. She had never heard this odd but really smart-ass comparison reference, but she got the idea, about life's pressures, when "you coulda had a V8" instead of being a shitty person.

"AND?!?"

"And I heard him exhale, a big sigh and then another big intake of air, and he thanked me. Then he said, "Well Leah I better go."

"So I blurted out what he was going to do with himself now?"

He said, "Well I'm not sure? I am not sure I can resolve anything."

"Oh wow, Charlie, what are you, fourteen? You are just going to get older and try to be better and maybe you'll succeed. Doubtful... but until you die, why not try to Fix Your Shit, as my Stepmom would say. And I said, there's always a V8."

"Oh my god Leasqueakabeah, you're so fabulous. Tell me you taped that call."

"I sure as hell did!"

I bought her a Bloody Mary. This joint had V8.

GREEN AND WHITE POLKA DOTS

Margaret had just left school and was thinking that people can be awful mean. She had watched her friend Alice being made fun of because she didn't know who the president was, like anyone wants to know that! Margaret asked if anyone cared who the president is, since everyone in class besides the teacher is ten or maybe eleven. Most everyone was thinking what the snack was after school. Mrs. Clark the teacher asked Margaret to take her seat, and said it was good and kind of her to protect her friend Alice, and we shouldn't make fun of others. But Margaret no longer cared about this. School was over, and she was outside the old building. She felt the new, warm, spring air and she felt wonderful. A few of the other girls were still around and asked if she wanted to play hopscotch and Margaret said "Nope". Her best friend Connie yelled "Big doings?" And a reply of "Yep Yep Yep" came from Margaret.

She was walking home by herself and it was the long sunlight and her impatience to get home to put on her old striped pinafore with the big pockets that she did not notice the man in the car across the street. But he pulled away when she happened to look up, and anyway she wasn't thinking about that.

Margaret ran the last block to her house, up the front steps and in the door directly to the kitchen. She changed her school shoes and put on her old sandals which she loved, grabbed her apron, the cookie left for her and tore out of the back door. Florence her mom and Jack her dad were at work. She knew to be home before dinner time.

On the back porch she sat down and ate half her cookie, a big oatmeal with ginger and raisins. Her mom baked every Wednesday. The cookies were for the whole week and at least two in everyone's lunch bag, so this being Tuesday, it wasn't as fresh but still delicious. Anyway, she'd help Saturday with her favorite of all, rice pudding... but her brain was fidgety and whispering "get up, let's move let's move." She ran down the back stairs and across the neighbor's yards and headed for the tracks and the field beyond.

In her pocket she had her "beautiful pale blue piece of glass, about five inches by maybe six inches?" stating it like a question to her friend Connie. Margaret had found it "Near the track yard where lots of junk or whatever had fallen or derailed or had just been thrown onto a big pile... not food trash, but solid stuff." Connie thought Maghee (the nickname she'd made up for her friend which drove Margaret crazy) was an amazing girl. "Oh Maghee, you are so darn brave, you have the oddest ideas and the best hikes and the funniest hobbies." Margaret thought the nickname was too boyish and she felt shy around the schoolboys who thought Margaret was pretty tough for a girl. But she loved her pal and let her use it and now everybody liked it, so, it was sort of nice to have a special name. Her dad loved it, said "It makes you standout and it gives you a special place in the town and with all the folks we know... it means you belong." Her dad Jack had not been born in the United States so belonging meant a lot to him so Margaret just sighed "Okay papa, I won't smack anyone who uses it."

As Margaret got nearer to the field she headed towards the narrow woods nearby to see if any spring flowers had come in yet. It was cooler and smelled richer there and as Margaret looked around, a breeze came up and made her shiver. Then she spied a little cache of Lady Slippers, and a few wild wood violets. She bent to pick some up and heard a little snap of noise... she turned, it was a brown rabbit, cute, chewing, and staring. She pulled two small lady slippers and about three violets and ran back out to the field. Margaret walked around until she found a spot she liked where the sun was still shining down to create her treasure box... digging a hole to put the flowers in and then putting the glass over it so she could look into the earth and watch the flowers, like a painting. She knew the flowers would only last so long and she would have to take them out or let them die. She laid on her side on her elbow so she could see the dreamy little garden and the sun made her sleepy...

Jack was finishing up at work. A machinist at the Little Falls Metal Works, he's well-liked and respected by his boss and the owners of the plant. He makes good pay and when he retires he will get a gold watch, and since arguing about a union has finally stopped, hopefully a pension, and there's talk Jack might teach the younger lads. Jack likes what he does, the precision and to be specific with his work. Makes him happy. Like his garden or his home projects, there is satisfaction. A pleasure where he is, and nothing reminding him of the passage to come over from England, so brutal, so lonely, and so far from Flossy.

Jack stared at the mirror where he used some oil to get the dirty oil off his hands and as he was cleaning up, the fellows asked if he wanted to get a beer or two. Jack thought for a moment but knew Flossie was making Hot Pot and he had to stop at the butchers to pick up the pork chops. "No boyos, Flossie will be waiting for the chops and Maghee's got a school project I'm helping her with..." His friend Ted reminded him that the league was playing tomorrow night and Jack "...you are gonna get the highest score and we are gonna take that trophy!." Jack laughed, waved and headed out. The fellows were attempting an early victory dance.

He hit the air, breathed deep and headed for the Butcher's. "My god, what a day. Everyone loves these sorts of days" he thought. He settled his mind on his walking and after a couple of blocks of enjoying the soft sunny air, he thought "I bet Maghee's with her 'windows...' Of all his children, Maghee was a puzzle. Shy but self-reliant, willful but kind, smart but too modest and fearless. "Where or who does that come from? Beatrice isn't like that at all..." and a thought flashed across his mind, "I don't actually like Bea, she's a stupid girl and hard to —What the Hell —I love my daughters and so what if Bea is, aah jesus Jack, christsakes and Russell is a damn good kid." Jack had to force his eyes into the sky to see the blue, and feel the warmth, deeply breathing again. He looked around at the neighborhood and returned to his walk, almost at the butcher's. He felt better. No Shell Shock, safe, fine a little wobbly but fine.

"Well damn, I could use a cold beer." He stopped at Hank's Butcher shop, had a short chat, got his chops and went next door to the Dew Drop Inn Tavern for a quick one. Jack would phone Florence so she wouldn't worry. On many an evening she would sit in his lap and soothe his head with her sweet chirping way.

As Jack past the field and the tracks he didn't see anyone, no Margaret, none of the other kids. He moved on and was coming up the road to his house. He liked his home, next to the river, good yard, sturdy and his. He climbed the front steps and heard Russell and Margaret arguing in the kitchen.

"Whaddayou mean shuck the corn... what kind of word is that?" Russell stared at Margaret as she rolled her eyes and said "It's pulling the silk off the corn so we can cook it without that string attached." "Oh" was all Russell could muster. "Well what kind of word is that - shuck?" Russell asked once more and Florence playing with the pans and potatoes and onions managed "You two stop this squabbling! Your dad will be here any minute and I for one would like to hear a sweet quiet with no squawking. And Russell, all the silk if you please, can't stand when it gets stuck in my teeth." "Yes mama."

"Margaret love, the milk and butter please..." "Yes mama" and in walked Jack.

Their evening was easy and calm and they finished so Jack could help Margaret with her little project. Making all the paper maché planets to go around the sun in a mobile thing. They had almost finished and Russell had fallen asleep in the big easy chair. Florence was doing a little bit of crocheting and the radio was near her playing a soft tune. "Jack" she said, "Will you carry the boy up?""Sure darlin'. Maghee, time for you too, come along."

Maghee and Jack with Russell over his shoulder climbed the stairs, she sprinting up backwards and Jack telling her to "Grab my bathrobe and slippers love". In the pretty bedroom where Florence kept her parasols and small sewing basket, Maghee put the robe on the bed and the slippers next to them. Jack came in with his shirt unbuttoned and underneath his old tee shirt was clean but mended. He pulled off the shirt and Margaret tossed it down the clothes shute. He put on his robe and said "Oh Maghee, look at this piece of glass I found at the tavern." It was a piece from a green bottle and Maghee was thrilled. She hugged her dad and took the downstairs steps two at a time to show her mom. Florence came up behind Margaret. Margaret's room was wall papered and she loved the window seat and the decorated dresser. She hugged her mother and Florence shut her door. With everyone settled in Florence finally closed the bedroom door and looked at her Jack and said, "Love, we are so lucky..." And all Jack could offer was "Come to bed Flossy."

The next day was gloriously sunny and Margaret was wearing her new green and white polka dot dress Florence had made. Even Connie and all the girls oohed and ahhed the beautiful shirring and tucks.

It was too warm so the kids were restless all day. Margaret couldn't wait for the end so she could use the new glass piece. She asked Connie if she wanted to go to the field with her to see the little show. The same car was outside the school when the day was done and this time Connie said that she had seen that car yesterday "Cause it's so shiny, like it's just been washed. Pretty isn't it?"

But Margaret was already moving and yelled "Hurry up!""Wait up Maghee" Connie called as she ran to catch up.

"Gotta stop at the house to get my apron and change my shoes and get us a cookie.""Okay" said Connie, "But I can't stay long, I have this awful book report for class tomorrow. I have to speak in front of the whole class, and I don't know how to write a report about a book I don't like."

"Well Connie, you could just say you didn't like the book so you stopped reading it after ten pages."

"Oh Maghee you are so funny..."

The girls got to Margarets' house, collected themselves, their cookies and tore off over to the field now deciding it should be known as "Maghees Meadow." When they arrived there were a few boys playing in the corner of the field but they weren't any problem and both girls found a beautiful bouquet for the hole. Connie asked "Maghee, don't you ever use clear glass?"

"Nope, I don't think that is as interesting or artistic as the colors all being smushed under the sun." And so they stared at the little glass show and Connie decided it was time to face the gruesome book report. She waved goodbye and headed off. By now the boys had also left and Margaret was alone.

Across the street was the shiny car and as Margaret was leaving the man driving the car waited for her to get nearer before asking her if she knew where the nearest pharmacy was or drugstore. Margaret didn't feel afraid and walked over to him and said, "Do you mean Greco's?" The man said "Oh, yes, I'm new here and want to pick up a few things for my house, do you know where that is?" "Sure do mister. It's not far from here at all, just a few blocks." The man offered Margaret a ride if she could show him how to get there and Margaret said that'd be good since it would get her closer to home. And she got into the car. She gave him directions to turn the car around which he did and then he drove and she asked him if he had any children. He stopped talking to her and said he had to pay attention to the road. As they neared the street where the village and drugstore was, Margaret saw the man pull his hat further down on his head and Margaret thought that was odd. The only light in town was on this street and when the light turned red the man didn't stop and Margaret yelled. The man grabbed at her but Margaret pulled away and pulled the handle of the door open and she jumped out and went tumbling and somersaulting on the pavement. Not that many cars were around and the man stopped his car and ran to get Margaret but she had gotten up started yelling and ran across the square into the drugstore still screaming, "He's after me, he's after me!!" The few people in the store ran outside to see what she meant but the car and the man had left. When the folks came back in they saw that the clerk had Margaret on the counter and was trying to calm her down. "He tried to pull at me and he's got a shiny shiny car and his hat is pulled way over his eyes and and he grabbed at me and you better get him!" The clerk called for Mr. Greco and finally the police were called. Margaret was given a cup of water and a piece of licorice and when the police arrived, they asked if she knew the man. "No, he was asking for directions to here and he offered to give me a ride so I did." The police looked at each other, there hadn't been much of this sort of thing so they were not sure what to do. Margaret kept shouting "Go get him, he's driving a shiny shiny car and he's got a hat!" Someone suggested they call Margaret's folks and get her to a doctor since she jumped out of a moving car. Mr. Greco asked if she was hurt or bleeding and remarkably she wasn't hurt at all. The shock would come later when her dad came and got her and her mom stopped crying and they asked if she was alright and then she looked down at her dress and started sobbing. It was torn and ripped and dirt was all over her new green and white polka dot dress and she sobbed in her mother's arms. Jack said they could fix the dress or make another one.

But from now on, Russell had to go everywhere Margaret went and she was never to take a ride from anyone except her dad and Connie's parents. And they asked her not to go to the field alone anymore. So Jack made a part of his garden for Maghee. She still collected glass and made little walls for the flowers and when Florence asked her if she wanted a new dress, Margaret said yes but not green and white polka dots. "Could it be white with yellow polka dots?" And Florence said yes.

AFTERWORD BY ELAINE BONOW

The NOCO Writers Workshop started in 2012 at the BBC (Belltown Ballet and Conditioning) studio in Belltown, an "innerburb" of Seattle. Ruth-Ellen Perlman, one of my ballet students, led the first group.

We wrote around 300 stories in our workshop there, until the building was sold in 2018.

After the move, the writers got lonely.

We unanimously decided to resurrect the group in September 2019 at Ola Wyola, a retail space I rent north of Columbia City. We kept our tradition of meeting on Tuesday evenings, including snacks and libations. This seemed perfect until our last in-person meeting on Feb. 23, 2020.

Mardi Gras signified the onset of the pandemic; and now we Zoom into our workshop like most of the online world.

We write for the sheer enjoyment of creating alternative universes, getting in touch with our subconscious selves. We encourage each other to write, even if we think we are too busy or can't think of anything to write.

We produced this book to inspire others to write, and so that our friends and family will think we are brilliant.

Elaine Bonow
Fearless Leader
NOCO Writers Workshop
wordpress.com/nocowriters.home.blog
(older stories: bbcstudiowrites.wordpress.com)

www.ingramcontent.com/pod-product-compliance
Lightning Source LLC
Chambersburg PA
CBHW070942250626
47159CB00009B/3346